I0683000

"Sweet, bid me hold my tongue,
    For in this rapture I shall surely speak
    The thing I shall repent."

William Shakespeare
Troilus and Cressida

RAPTURES

Tales of Darkness & Light

Charles Watts

Ra Press
100 Kennedy Drive #53
South Burlington, VT 05403
www.rapressrafilms.com

The following stories were originally published in
literary journals, magazines, or anthologies. All Hail
the small presses of the world. They are our voice.

The Hunt: Bactrian Room, Dec. 2011
Under the Bugala Moon: Writers' Bloc, July 2010
Hotel Peshawar: Liebamour, Jan. 2011
Gone Fishing: Road Poets, RA Press Anthology, 2011
The River: Commonline Journal, Feb. 2011
The Accidental Touron: Adirondack Life, Feb. 2012

The author photograph was taken at Bluseed Studios,
Saranac Lake, NY by Shaun Ondak

Copyright 2012
Charles Watts
All rights reserved
ISBN-13: 978-0615686653

beat writers adirondack series

CONTENTS

ABNEGATION

None of the characters in this book are real people. If you feel one or more of them reflect you in some negative way, I suggest a vegan diet, counseling, or a strong naturopathic laxative. You'll feel better in the morning.

STOLEN PREFACE

It's curious that we can't possibly tell what exactly will be considered great and important, and what will seem paltry and ridiculous. Did not the discoveries of Copernicus or Columbus, let us say, seem useless and ridiculous at first, while the nonsensical writings of some wiseacre seemed true? Man has been endowed with reason, with the power to create, so that he can add to what he's been given. But up to now, he hasn't been a creator, only a destroyer. Forests keep disappearing, rivers dry up, wild life becomes extinct, the climate is ruined, and the land grows poorer and uglier. Time will pass, and we shall go away forever, and we shall be forgotten, our faces will be forgotten, our voices, and how many there were of us; but our sufferings will pass into joy for those who will live after us, happiness and peace will be established upon earth, and they will remember kindly and bless those who have lived before.

Happiness does not await us all. One needn't be a prophet to say that there will be more grief and pain than serenity and money. That is why we must hang on to one another. You ask "What is life?" That is the same as asking "What is a carrot?" A carrot is a carrot and we know nothing more.

We shall find peace. We shall hear angels. We shall see the sky sparkling with diamonds.

(This preface is a remix of Anton Chekhov quotes)

PROLOGUE:

RAPTURES

written on May 21, 2011
the Day of Rapture not-to-be
for Harold Camping

In the year of his lord 44
Theudas declared himself Messiah
And fled to the desert with 400 faithful.
Roman soldiers beheaded him
And his soul rose to heaven, leaving
His followers behind, scattered in the dust,
A day like any other

In more or less 1000, Charlemagne's body
Was exhumed on Pentecost, the great king
Risen to forestall the apocalypse sure
To come at the end of the millennium.
The Caliph Al Hakim sacked the
Holy Sepulcher in Zion to mock
The date, igniting a violent round
Of anti-Jewish pogroms in the West,
A year like any other

The sun did not turn red or rain
Tears of blood or fail to shine
Plague and death did not follow
No new comets were sighted in the heavens
The moon harvested a bushel of stars,
A night like any other

Witnesses from a Watchtower saw
The invisible return of some virgin
Born being in 1914, 1918, 1920, 1925
1941, 1975, 1994 and today at six
In the afternoon in Jerusalem,
A town like any other

The yard is a bloom of dandelions
The dog yelps at a neighbor up the hill
A rain shower came and went and came
Again. It is sunny now, and I can see
My skin has gone white from the long winter
Summer will return my tan, oh evensong will bring
A darkness like any other

LOUNGE LIZARD

My flight into Albany was filled with odd persons. The flight attendant had breasts the size of muskmelons, breasts that defied gravity, breasts that someday will fall and touch her navel. I am cursed this way. When I look at a woman, I see her as she will look at 64. This character flaw has caused me to miss many opportunities for anonymous sex with currently good looking women. I did not hit on her.

My seatmate was an engineer of some sort, dropping off his wife with relatives in upstate New York before heading out to meetings with oil companies in London and Paris. Then he was off to Kabul. His company wanted to build a pipeline from land of the Uzbeks to the Indian Ocean, and Afghanistan was in the way. It was his fervent hope that the locals could be tamed or cowed or killed or controlled by our mighty fighting forces so he could bribe the proper Afghan officials and make lots of money and retire early. His porcine wife, in the window seat eating what appeared to be a homemade sandwich of canned ham and yellow plasticine cheese, only smiled when I asked if she feared for his safety.

"God will protect him," she said. "Besides, he has insurance."

There was a bus from the airport to Lake Placid, but I got off in Keene Valley. A fellow passenger said the pie was good at the Noon Mark Diner, and I had not eaten since boarding the plane; a hot country meal capped with raspberry pie sounded worth the detour.

The restaurant was almost full. At one table, a man sat alone. He was wearing a tight green full body wet suit, complete with hoody, and a pair of trashed work boots with duct tape on the steel toes. No one in the diner seemed to take notice. I asked if I could join him. His name was Larry. He ordered a hamburger and cherry-peach pie. He was on his way to rehearse a play at the Recovery Lounge in Upper Jay, the apparent locus of high culture in these mountains. I ordered chicken fried steak and the raspberry crumb pie and asked if I could go along. I like plays.

In its first incarnation, the Recovery Lounge assembled Model T Fords on a low bank above the Ausable River. During this time as a manufacturing facility, the value of hard labor was the lesson the building had to learn. Later, in the 30's and 40's, it was reborn as an incubator of forests, spent its days shaking pine cones and bagging the seeds for sale to the lumber farming aristocracy, a group of railroad magnates devoted to the nurture and execution of trees for the burgeoning suburban housing market. The building learned to hold its tongue. In the latter decades of the 20th century, a group of artisans and middle aged hippies turned it into an antique and craft co-op. This venture died as children were born and money and real jobs became an issue for the fertile and passionate artists. The building learned how to love. Most of this I heard from one of the current inhabitants, an actor and upholstery artist from New Jersey.

His name was Albert, and what he said was this: "It was an assembly plant for Model T's, a seed store, and an antique emporium." The rest I learned from the bricks and mortar. I am getting better at communicating with inanimate objects.

In its current birth, the Recovery Lounge was learning about multiple personality disorder. During the day, she was the best, perhaps the only, upholstery shop in the Adirondacks. Albert and his brother Mark, a recovering born again Christian alt indie bass player, had abandoned the urbane dream of success in the arts and fame in the city for this crumbling artifact of the industrial age, a place to escape the madness and engage in a simple and honorable trade. Albert never said where he learned to do upholstery. He was one of those rare beings who did not take his identity from his job title.

At night, the sewing machines and half-finished furniture were pushed aside to create a performance space. Incense was lit and pipes filled with various exotic substances and liquor swigged. The upholstery shop misted off into the shadows and a new mistress arose to dominate the spirit of the building by the river, a bawdy hooker rolling her buttocks at the passing cars and inviting the corrupt and creative to come on in, slump into a lumpy recliner, and get down and dirty with the music or poetry or dance troupe or play or whatever Albert planned for the night.

This evening a group had gathered to rehearse some drama involving lizards. Larry took off his work boots and strapped on a six foot long articulated tail of Styrofoam and wire painted green. The female lizard was played by Saint Amanda of the Hard On, for that was my reaction when she walked in the door. She was small and fox like, legs cocked in a hunting crouch, ready to leap. Eyes that flashed like Leopard Moths dancing face first into an incandescent light. Cheeks so sunken she could be screaming on a bridge. Her tail was only four feet long, but it was good enough for me.

Albert was directing the lizards as they crawled over sand dunes of cotton batting covered with burnt Siena muslin. They approached humans sunbathing on beach towels a few feet from the empty audience chairs. Larry oozed in slowly to sniff the curious creatures, disturbing their mindless reverie. The humans leapt up screaming. The lizards ran back over the dune. "Cut!" shrieked Albert.

"Look, lizards. You have tails. Use them. Larry, stand here. Amanda, there."

Larry and Amanda went to their marks, and Albert told them to shake their butts from side to side, to get those tails moving. Amanda swung her hips slowly, dancing in her head to a downbeat love song involving loss and a three legged Chihuahua. I'm guessing about the Chihuahua. My ability in mind wave reading from living subjects is far less developed than my numinous connection to inanimate objects, so the dog may be a misinterpretation. Forgive me.

Larry was less successful. His hip thrusts were so

violent and powerful that the tail was ripped from his rump and flew across the room, just missing Albert's head. I looked away for a moment, distracted by a deer head floating in the clouds of pot and patchouli forming at the margins of the ceiling, and when I turned back, the tail had grown a new Larry. These are magic mountains.

Take two: The lizards crawled over sand dunes of cotton batting covered with burnt Siena muslin. They approached humans sunbathing on beach towels a few feet from the empty audience chairs. Larry oozed in slowly to sniff the curious creatures, disturbing their mindless reverie. The humans leapt up screaming. The lizards ran back over the dune, swinging their tails wildly. Larry spun for one more look at the beach creatures, and his lashing tail caught Amanda smack between the shoulder blades. She dropped like an unpopular Lieutenant shot in the back by his own troops and lay on the stage in a green lump.

When she returned to the conscious world, she had no tales of strange travels through tunnels of light, only a monster headache. I told her I could help. I asked permission to touch her neck and shoulders. She blessed me with a yes. I found the offending pressure points at the base of her cranium and under her scapula and manipulated her energy flow to purge the damaged area and give it peace. Her aura turned from muddy red to green to blue. I was waiting for the gratitude and passion colors when her tall and young and handsome husband strolled through the door to pick her up. Tonight, at least, we were not to be.

Larry was black with guilt. His physical expression of this involved loud denunciations of his fanny flapping ways and long pulls from a jug of Johnny Walker Red. It was soon clear he was not competent to drive home that night. Albert offered us the sand dune.

I could not sleep. Larry snored softly in the darkness, an even, alcohol modulated rumble in the mostly silent night. I focused on the deer head on the wall. It was real, a dead thing hung in the border between darkness and light, a pure and nonjudgmental witness to the happenings of lizards and humans and Model T Fords. And seeds of the pine cone.

Larry began sleep talking words of love to someone named William. He rolled over in his sleep and nuzzled against me, his hand on my leg. "William, please, one more time. Just one...." I pushed him gently away, found the lizard tails and placed them between us. Sleep finally came.

THE HUNT

Karim heard his father moving around the room, but pretended to be asleep. He did not want it thought that he was the kind to lie awake in the night and worry. When his father left the room, Karim crawled deeper under the warm cotton quilt and pushed his feet against the charcoal brazier. His mother turned in her sleep, softly touching his feet with hers. It had been cold that night, and the whole family spread their covers over the low table in the center of the room, slid the brazier under the table, and lay down to sleep. Their bodies radiated out from the table like the spokes of Uncle Mustapha's bicycle.

Karim could hear his father praying in the garden. He rose quietly, careful not to disturb his sisters, and washed his hands and face. He took a small prayer carpet from behind the door and joined his father. He faced his carpet to the southwest, toward Mecca, knelt and recited the scriptures of the morning.

Uncle Mustapha arrived while the women were preparing tea. Karim's father opened the gate for him, and Uncle Mustapha wheeled his sparkling new Chinese bicycle into the garden. It was the only bicycle in the village, and Karim was proud to be the nephew of the man who owned it. Often, at the new mud schoolhouse the government built the year before, he told his classmates of being thrown from side to side as the old man careened down the dusty alleys of the village. Uncle Mustapha brought the bicycle from Tehran on top of a bus. Karim met him where the dirt track that led to the village began and rode the last ten kilometers home clinging to his uncle's back. Uncle Mustapha's long mustaches flapped in the wind like a flock of pigeons coming to the roost.

The two old men greeted each other formally. Uncle Mustapha bowed slightly and placed his right hand over his heart. "May God be with you, Haji." "Thank you, my brother. May God walk with you." Karim ignored the men and looked at the bicycle. "Where are you, boy? Your Uncle needs tea!"

Karim shook himself aware and fetched the tea. His father, the Haji, was not a man to be crossed. He was the only man in the village who had made the pilgrimage to Mecca, the only man entitled to be called Haji. Short and broad, enormously strong, he was the best hunter in the mountains, and Karim often sat at Uncle Mustapha's feet in the evenings and heard tales of his father's exploits.

Today they would be hunting for a wolf pup. The Haji wanted to breed it to one of the village dogs and see if it could be taught to protect the sheep against its full blood wolf brothers. Several lambs had been lost that year, and the village was poor. Karim, at twelve years old, would not normally have gone on a wolf hunt. He had been out hunting with his father many times, it was true, but always after tamer game, rabbits and birds. For wolf pups, however, a small body was needed, small enough to crawl in a cave and gather the young after the mother had been killed. Karim had gone over it all in his dreams, the darkness, the fearful whimpering of the pups turning into growls as he reached for them in the visionless abyss, the possibility of snakes or scorpions or spiders, and he had almost convinced himself that he was not afraid.

Uncle Mustapha and the Haji prepared to leave while Karim cleared the rug of tea implements. Uncle Mustapha slipped his long skinning knife into the broad sash around his waist and straightened his turban. His baggy trousers and tight, almost military-style shirt was a style seldom seen these days. Most of the villagers, even Karim, wore modern trousers and shirts, but the Haji and his brother preferred the old Kurdish style. Though they dressed the same, the Haji looked somehow more modern, more attuned to the new world of electricity and transistor radios. His M-16 rifle, smuggled in by the Kurds fighting for their freedom across the border in Iraq, shone in a dim corner, a symbol of the new world. Uncle Mustapha also had a gun, an old Enfield from the time of the British, but he seldom used it. He said he preferred to feel the life flowing out of his victims at close quarters, that to kill at a distance was an insult to the power of the spirit of living things, a discourtesy and an insult. The Haji had no time for such views. He had a family to support, and every year saw less and less game in the hills, more and more people in the village. If a man were to feed three growing daughters and a son, he did what was called for by circumstance. Tradition was for those who could afford such luxuries.

The two men, followed by the boy, left the village an hour before full dawn and were soon marching single file into the hills, brown and lifeless in the distance, but full of hidden springs and sudden patches of green close up. In the higher hills, snow still lay in the shadows, and here the ground was wet from the rains, making footholds difficult. The older men knew these hills from boyhood, knew each boulder and twist of the path. Karim carefully put his feet in the prints left by his father and his uncle. He, too, had grown up in these hills, had stood on the great ridge above the village and sent his voice echoing down the valley, had set snares among the rocks for grouse and partridge. But today was different, today he must make no errors, today he could not be a boy.

The sun broke as they crossed the second group of peaks, and Karim was sure he could see to the end of the mountains. Streams flashed dull grey down the steep beige hillsides, down to the villages below, studded with the blue domes of small mosques and shrines. Over the next set of hills there were no villages, no life but the wild creatures God had given man to fill his belly. It was cruel and it was necessary, death to feed life. It was necessary and therefore unworthy of thought. It was.

They saw no game for several hours. The morning was clear and crisp, the first rainless day in weeks. Karim was happy to have the sun on his face, to be here with his father and uncle rather than at home, stuck with his mother and sisters, forced to be civil and polite, to sit in the courtyard and study his lessons for the following week, to draw water like a girl for the midday meal. He looked to the west and thanked God that he was allowed to be here, free, doing a man's work in these ancient mountains. Karim smiled at the sun.

Uncle Mustapha stopped suddenly and peered into the distance.

"Haji, look. The birds are circling."

"Let's go and see."

The buzzards were turning slowly in the sky about a mile away, working lazy turns over the death of some creature, waiting for the final convulsions, the last moments of weakness. They would not wait for complete death, of course. They would come in when the animal was sufficiently weak to not fight back, tear out its living flesh in great steaming hunks.

It was a deer, a big male with small, beautifully branched horns. He stood, blood running down his chest and neck, surrounded by three wolves. One, a large male, probably the leader of the pack, darted around the head of the deer, leaping forward and then back, distracting the deer from the others. A smaller wolf jumped on the deer from behind and tore another great gash in its neck, then pulled back and continued to circle.

The Haji lifted his rifle. When he pulled the trigger, the sound of the explosion filled the air completely, gathered to itself the full attention of each sentient creature in the area. It seemed to Karim that the big wolf looked at him for a split second just before the bullet smashed into its face.

The other wolves stared at the hunters for a moment, then trotted off down a small meadow and around a group of boulders. Karim watched his father aim again. This time the deer fell. Uncle Mustapha skinned the two animals quickly and rolled the pelts into a neat package. Karim put them in the back pack he had brought for the purpose.

"What about the meat, Haji?"

"Leave it for the birds for now."

The Haji started off in the direction the wolves had taken, then abruptly turned uphill. He stopped in the shade of a small tree and sat.

"They'll come back for the meat. We'll wait here."

The men and the boy sat quietly and watched the birds drop greedily out of the sky onto the carcasses, watched them pound their beaks into the gore and come up, blood rolling down their wrinkled, featherless heads. The birds fought each other for the best morsels, though there was enough for all.

Uncle Mustapha put his hand on Karim's shoulder and pointed. The two wolves had moved out of the rocks and were approaching the dead animals. They sniffed the air for human scent, but the hunters were downwind. They leapt among the birds, snarling and tearing with their teeth at the fleeing scavengers. The small male fell upon the body of the deer. The female gnawed the dead wolf.

The Haji raised his rifle and fired again. This time the young male fell. The female looked at the men but did not move. Karim's father cocked the gun but didn't shoot. After several seconds, she trotted off.

Uncle Mustapha skinned the young wolf and gave the pelt to Karim.

"It is a good day, Master Karim. Three skins will bring enough rice for a month."

"But why didn't he kill the female?"

"Do you question your father? He's not a man to act without a reason."

"But he could have shot it."

Uncle Mustapha smiled and turned away. "Come. Let's find your father."

The Haji had already begun following the last wolf and was far in the distance by the time Karim and his uncle started after him. They walked quickly but silently up the muddy hill to where the solid rock began. The Haji stopped near a small outcropping and waited for them.

"I was too late. She went into her cave. See up there?" He pointed at a small hole in the side of the rocks above, barely perceptible. "She will stay as long as we are here. We have to bring her out."

He looked at his son with a smile on his lips. "Karim, come here. I have work for you."

Karim looked at his father, but didn't move. Uncle Mustapha pushed him lightly from behind and he walked stiffly to his father. The Haji took off his turban and unwrapped the long cotton cloth. He tore it into two strips, took several strong branches from a nearby tree, and bound them with the cloth around his son's hands and arms.

"When you enter the cave, you must keep your

arms in front of you. When she leaps, she'll take your arm in her mouth. She won't let go. We'll drag you both out and kill her. Then you can go back for the pups. Are you ready?"

"Yes, father."

They walked to the mouth of the small cave. Karim tried to appear calm and brave, like when he had ridden on the bicycle with Uncle Mustapha, but the blood was crashing in his ears. He looked at the hole, barely large enough for his tiny shoulders. Oh father, do not make me do this, he whispered in his heart.

Uncle Mustapha touched his shoulder. "Today you will have your fourth skin."

Karim had no trouble slipping the upper half of his body into the opening. He heard the mother wolf growling nearby in the darkness. His body blocked the small light of the entrance, and he could not even make out her eyes. He had dreamed they would flash like flint on steel. He could feel the hands of his father and uncle as they gripped his legs, ready to pull when the time came.

Karim inched forward on his belly, keeping his arms out as a shield. The female wolf gave a low growl and leapt, slashing down on his raised arms with her great teeth. He could feel the fangs crushing the branches protecting him, working deeper and deeper toward the flesh. He could feel himself being dragged backward out of the cave, feel his head and shoulders banging into the narrow rocks of the entrance. The wolf clung to him.

Then he was out in the air and he could see her face, full of hate and fear and death, inches from his own. For a moment time slowed. He saw the wolf release him and turn. The Haji had his knife in one hand and was reaching for the beast. She caught his knife hand above the wrist and ripped out half the flesh. Uncle Mustapha grabbed the animal by the tail and tried to pull her off the Haji, but it turned on him and in one lunge had him by the throat. The Haji took the knife in his good hand and plunged it time and again into the back and breast of the wolf.

She fell, shuddering in the mud to her death. It was too late for Uncle Mustapha. His windpipe hung from the tear in his neck, and bright bubbles of blood were oozing from the wound. Karim took the cloth that had protected him from the wolf and wrapped it around his father's arm. The Haji stared at his brother with empty eyes. He did not move and he did not weep.

"Karim, go home and bring back some men."

Karim turned away from the Haji and walked toward the cave.

"I told you to go and bring men!"

Karim looked at the Haji, and then at Uncle Mustapha. "I will, father." He crawled back into the cave, heard the growling. He reached into the darkness, grabbed a pup by the neck and dragged it out, snarling and spitting and clawing at his arms.

When Karim returned with the men of the village, the Haji was still standing silently beside his brother. It took several hours to carry Uncle Mustapha back home over the mountains, but the Haji never spoke. An almost full moon lit the way. They arrived after midnight. The body rested on the kitchen table.

It was the duty of the closest male relatives to clean and prepare the dead for burial. The Haji took a needle and thread and sewed up the wound in Uncle Mustapha's neck, so he would look whole before God. He and Karim placed a cloth on the body, poured water over it, and cleaned off the blood of the day. They wrapped Uncle Mustapha in the Kafan, a long white cotton shroud, and called the men to come and take Uncle Mustapha to his grave. The dawn burial was quiet, for when Mohammed's son died, the Prophet said, "The eyes shed tears and the heart is grieved, but we will not say anything except that which pleases our Lord."

As they walked back to the house, the Haji finally spoke to Karim.

"What did you do with the pup?"

Karim led his father to the back garden of the house. An old bitch with her own pups was suckling the wolf. The Haji grabbed the wolf pup by the neck and tore it off the teat. With his free hand he pulled the knife from his cummerbund and held the pup high above his head, silhouetted in the rising sun.

It seemed the Haji held the pup for all of time. Karim wanted to scream "No!" but he could do nothing. He had already defied his father once that day, and did not have the strength left in him. He turned away and fell to his knees. The tears came, but he did not cry out.

The Haji looked down at his son. He dropped his knife in the dirt and put the pup back on the teat. He picked up his son and set him on his feet.

"Come."

They walked together to the front garden. The Haji pointed at Uncle Mustapha's bicycle.

"I can never ride it. It's yours."

The Haji returned to the back garden and sat slumped in the dust beside the dogs and wolf. Karim stared at the bike for a moment, then joined his father.

UNDER THE BUGALA MOON

Dr. Emami has his happy face on. That means he wants me to do something. I don't like to do things.

I like to smoke some opium and lay back and read a book and go to class and improvise a lesson. I like to visit Sufi shrines and Zoroastrian fire temples on the weekends, and to go on picnics under Mulberry trees by streams flowing through barren hills with my Iranian friends. I like to fanaticize about Dr. Emami's wife Jennie. She speaks Farsi with a South Carolina accent and has long black hair and wears long tight jeans and has been entirely too friendly as of late. I am grateful.

But I don't like to do things, especially for the good doctor. Last time he came in looking like this, I had to teach my Iranian colleagues how to play baseball. They were crappy players. They had grown up kicking soccer balls and didn't know how to use their arms. They threw like girls and batted like little leaguers, eyes closed and chin in the air. But they could run like a rainstorm on the desert. In one game, we had three inside the park home runs on soft grounders. Pitiful.

Dr. Emami loves everything American. He got his Ph.D. in literature at the University of South Carolina in the '60s, and went back to Iran with his dark haired South Carolina student bride just as the Shah began opening two or three Universities every year. By the time I was hired, he was head of the English Department at the new University in Kerman, his home town, on the edge of the desert that connects Iran, Afghanistan and Pakistan.

He stole me away from a cushy Lit job at the University in Shiraz. My wife had just left with the jerk in the apartment upstairs, and I did not relish coming back to a new semester after the summer vacation. Whispers in the hallway. Another expatriate that can't keep his wife in line. The divorce rate is high for foreigners here. Dr. Emami made the offer at a conference in Tehran. Better to make a clean start in a place where I'm not known.

My first mission was to bring in some Americans for the English Department. That was easy. Times were tough in the '70's, and lots of academics were out of work. I made a few calls to a friend at the University of South Carolina and got two couples with Masters, a British woman with a Doctorate in Urban Folklore, and a gay guy with a degree in teaching English as a foreign language. Signed, sealed and delivered to the Iranian desert in two months flat. Did I mention I am a graduate of USC? I wasn't hired for my looks.

Today Dr. Emami is on a saccharine yet somehow poignant mission. He wants me to organize a traditional American Thanksgiving celebration for the Iranian staff, complete with turkeys and cranberries and mashed potatoes and gravy. And hot eggnog with Johnny Walker Black. He has a case stashed for just such an occasion.

Cranberries. I'd have to ship them in from Minnesota or some damn place, and it takes three weeks for an aerogram to make it to Tehran, much less the USA. It's a week before the holiday. Not going to happen. Emami doesn't care. The party's at his place on the 27th. Get enough turkey for 40. Most of the faculty is coming.

I don't like to do things. I call a meeting of the foreign staff. Dan and Julie are responsible for turkeys. I tell them to order seven and to get a couple of local volunteers to help cook. Dr. Emami lives in an old style house, with rooms arranged around a garden. The kitchen is separate, with modern stoves and a 100 year old beehive shaped oven for cooking bread. That's Iran. Comfortable with both the old and the new.

Mark and Stacy are assigned potatoes and pumpkins. They're a little slow, but both veggies are available in the bazaar, so I figure no problem. The gay guy suggests cute little multicolored corn cobs. I assign him the centerpiece. Duty done.

Except for Roxy. Roxanne. Roxy.

Roxanne is the Brit. She keeps asking people to call her Roxy, but nobody can. She dresses like your maiden Aunt, with long peasant skirts of India cotton and tight little vests over her tight little breasts. She is smart and jolly and oblivious to the world around her. Her first week in Kerman she bought a bike and rode down the main street to the bazaar to shop. You'd have thought the Whore of Baghdad wheeled in. People scattered to avoid her presence. She thought they were being polite. Two months in and she still rides the bike. Oblivious. I tell her she can help cook.

I'll do the nog and Johnny.

Comes the day. Dan and Judy say the turkeys are to be delivered at noon, so everybody else is there by 11:30, except the Iranians who are supposed to help in the kitchen. They stroll in at one. Still no turkeys. Dr. Emami and Jennie show up, he with the booze and she with some kind of Black Widow outfit on, midnight cotton pajamas and a scarlet vest. She is here to help in any way she can.

A banging at the gate. I look through the peep door and see the head of some peasant. He says the bugalamuns are here. An hour and a half late and the turkeys finally arrive. If they're still frozen, we'll barely have time to cook them before dinner. Bummer. I open the gate and in gobble seven live birds.

I scream at Dan and Judy. They claim they ordered them frozen. Never trust a newcomer to get it right. I killed some chickens at Grandma's farm back when I was a kid, but seven turkeys are well beyond my skill set. None of the other Americans had ever seen a turkey except at the petting zoo.

Roxanne and the Iranian women come to the rescue. Turns out she was raised on a farm in Sussex and has country chops. Farideh, Dr. Emami's niece from a nearby village his family owns, organizes the Iranian women and gets huge pots of water on the fire. Roxanne chases down the turkeys with the help of a couple of servant boys and lops off their heads with a butcher knife and a quick twist. The headless main entrees run around and finally collapse in the dirt of the courtyard. The Iranian women dip them in and out of the caldrons of boiling water and yank out clumps of feathers. Roxanne puts on an apron and sharpens a knife. Today she's wearing a long white cotton skirt with a loose lime green top. There's blood and mud on her skirt. She doesn't seem to care. In fact, she seems happy.

Mark and Stacy got the veggies right. The gay guy... I am such a secret homophobe, curse me. Harry somehow found small corncobs and painted them in festive orange and black and blue. The centerpiece weighs at least 15 pounds. He made individual decorations for 60 place settings, just in case extra people came by. Clearly a go to gay guy.

Jennie helps me carry the Johnny Walker into the kitchen area. Twelve bottles of hundred dollar scotch. I think about stashing one in my shoulder bag, but there are too many witnesses. Jennie grabs a couple of the Iranian faculty wives and starts whipping up the egg yolks and cream and milk and honey and nutmeg. You have to heat it slow or the yolks will cook up and ruin the whole batch. Add the JW at the end, just in case They dump the mash into a large pot and start stirring. Jennie washes her hands, smiles, leans over and whispers in my ear. Am I interested in a joint?

I haven't smoked with any of the university people here, except the Americans. I guess my reputation as a doper followed me from Shiraz. No one seems to care as long as I keep to myself and say nothing about the Shah. All the off campus Iranians I know smoke hash and opium. I do try to be careful around work. Still. Midnight black pajamas. Hot hash.

There's an empty guest bedroom out by the garden. We slip in and spread out one of the rolled up futon style mattresses stored in the corner, prop up a couple of pillows against the wall, lounge down and light up. I don't know how long we're in there, but some kind of nipple erection experiment is going down when Dr. Emami walks in. Our clothes are still on, but nothing else about the situation can be interpreted as innocent.

Emami sits down. Jennie offers him a joint. He does not look loose and happy. He takes a hit, takes Jennie's hand, hands me the joint and leads her out of the room. Not a word. I suspect it's happened before. Probably worse. Certainly worse. She waives and blows me a kiss as she leaves.

Not much of a man, but he's my boss.

I go back to the kitchen. A damned disaster. Dr. Emami had come by after his wife and I disappeared, saw the case of scotch on the ground by the stove, knew in his heart that it would be stolen if left there, had the cooks pour it into the bubbling caldron of eggnog mash, and went looking for us. The nog was bubbling because it was too hot. The egg yolks turned into a gelatinous mass of yellow crud. Twelve hundred bucks of Johnny Walker Black down the drain. Man or not, Dr. Emami would not be amused.

Roxanne comes to the rescue. She scrapes the egg

mass out, has the women folk strain the remains of the liquid through a tablecloth, tells them to chop up some lamb and fat, and says to give her fifteen minutes. She jumps on her bike and by god in 14 minutes flat she's back in the kitchen with a dozen limes, a jar of cloves, and a bottle of Angostura Bitters. No way to get that here, so she must have brought it with. Not the first thing I would have thought to bring with me to a job in an exotic and foreign land, but who am I to judge? I brought a suitcase full of blue jeans to barter for Middle Eastern gold. I couldn't give them away. Good Chinese knockoffs cost three bucks.

She juices half the limes and slices the rest. She pours in the bitters and lime juice, sticks cloves into the lime slices and floats them on top. Voila. Hot Toddy. A bit eggy, but drinkable.

She takes fist sized bits of the scotch boiled eggs and covers them with a layer of lamb sausage, rolls them in bread crumbs, and dips them in boiling oil. Appetizers.

Farideh puts herself in charge of the kitchen and sends us home to change for the party. She is 17 and has those wide Scheherazade eyes that sing to you from behind the veil. "I am here, I am young and nubile, I could be yours for a pistachio and a pomegranate." She might be my student next year. Sweet.

I go home and change into a white cotton tab collar shirt, white cotton drawstring pants, and pull back my hair into a slick Bollywood ponytail. I smoke some opium and mellow out. Back to the party.

The sun is just setting through the grape arbor at the back of Dr. Emami's garden. Lights are strung up in the palms and persimmon trees. An enormous wooden buffet stretches for 20 meters, rose bushes on every side. The turkeys are perfect and brown and march down the table like ducks in a sideshow shooting gallery. Harry's center piece and place settings are a stunning success. Farideh and her crew ferry out steaming bowls of mashed potatoes and yams with tamarind sauce and pitchers of gravy and platters of scotched Scotch Eggs. The hot toddy is widely lauded and quickly drunk. The pumpkin pies have a hint of clove.

The table somehow disappears and the music starts. Iranians love to dance, and the garden is instantly full of writhing bodies, arms and chins in the air and legs doing a modified Middle Eastern mambo. The Dance of the Bugalamun.

A silver crescent rises behind the garden's trees, a headless turkey scrambling blindly through the branches of the night. A circle of dancers forms, with Farideh in the center spinning and clapping her hands. Jennie joins her. Like lovers in a duel, they spar with their hips and breasts. Harry jumps in and wows the crowd with a sultry Belly Dance. A young professor from Engineering joins him. The circle breaks and everyone is out there, dancing under the Bugala Moon. Roxanne and I.... Roxy and I glide to each other without a glance.

HOTEL PESHAWAR

It was over 100 degrees and 90 percent humidity, a nice way of saying that we, the trees, the cops, the hotel staff, the stray dogs, were wasted and up to nothing. Roxy and I lay on separate braided rope beds with thin cotton mattresses, naked, soaking up the small breeze created by the ceiling fan. The flies began to die of the heat.

I tried to think about the bus trip from Afghanistan, the Khyber Pass, the border crossing into Pakistan, but it was all gone. I tried to give my last chunk of hash away before I left Kabul, but nobody at the hotel wanted it. They all had plenty. It was eat it or toss it. I was so stoned on the bus ride to Peshawar that I remembered virtually nothing. Roxy had somehow gotten me through customs. Cost her five rupees and a body search by a Pakistani border guard with a hard on. She was not happy.

The level of my own thoughts was not high. They said to me, "Have a smoke." I never smuggle and I hadn't had time to score. There's always something on the other side of the border. I decided, considering the heat, to get semi-dressed and go down to the restaurant. I wrapped a rag around my waist, slipped on a white Nehru vest, asked Roxy if she wanted anything ("God yes, but they don't have it here"), and headed down with tea and dope on my mind.

The restaurant was a large, high-ceilinged room with blue plaster walls, scarred wooden tables covered with clear plastic sheets, and a few hippies and local Pakistanis hanging around drinking tea. The hippies were the real deal, not your Hollywood storybook make love not war peace out pussies. There were tall skinny French morphine freaks looking for a hotel near nowhere to die, Spanish anarchists trying to decide whether or not to go home and answer their draft notices, Dutch henna heads with long purple hair and sitars across their backs, the true heirs of the Dadaists and beatniks and hippies and hermit hard asses of history, 1970's Asia Silk Road Style.

One identifying mark is the way they sit. All true members of the tribe have dysentery. It's a point of honor to do things the local way, to merge with the local, to eat the local. Throwing caution and our kindergarten sanitation training to the winds, we feast on infested Kabobs, break teeth on roasted street corner corn cobs, gorge on Kabuli Polo and clutch our guts in the rancid Pakistani night. We ignore the proverb that states, "If the raisins move, don't eat them."

In the restaurant I saw a familiar face, a Dutch exotica dealer we met in Herat a few weeks back. His name was J. Edgar and he dealt in bones. He had Yak bone perfume jars from Tibet, goat bone trumpets from Nepal, a bowl made from a human skull carved with the hair of Shiva, cigarette holders of camel and cow, ivory bracelets brown and cracked with age, and he loved each piece as if it were his brother. It burned his soul to sell them in Amsterdam to people who could understand their history but never their value, sell them to be displayed on a shelf with a note in calligraphy about their age and origin. "Oh yes, it's one of a kind."

And paid him pretty fine. He was on the road 350 days a year. When a man is at peace, his life becomes simple, the categories he lives by become fewer and less rigorous. So it was with J. Edgar. To him you were either a capitalist or a free man, out there, searching for the end of the road.

Luckily, he intuited that I was mostly like him, a bum, even though I had a teaching job nine months of the year. He told me this one night in Herat when we took acid in the garden of the hotel. It was the night we met. We were watching either Jupiter or Saturn cruising just to the left of the moon. Roxy was in the toilet vomiting up her Kabuli Polo. J. Edgar took a deep toke on his joint, coughed it out, looked me in the eye and said: "Phil, why the fuck did you bring a woman to this filthy and dangerous part of the world?"

My Dad couldn't have said it straighter. Being on acid, I wasn't up for metaphysics, natural theology or morals, especially the morals part, so I took the coward's way and said, "I told her what to expect, J. Edgar. She's a grown woman. Don't you worry."

J. Edgar said: "Phil, you're a bum."

By this time, I was a touch irritated. "J," I said, "I don't need a damn trinket dealer lecturing me. She asked to come along and she can leave if she damn well pleases."

J. Edgar said: "Would you let her? You know what happens to women who travel alone. You are a perfect example of ...." J. Edgar phased out, took another hit, and returned to his study of the planets.

Now, in Peshawar, J. Edgar looked a little burned out. "Dysentery," he said. "Three weeks in Kashmir with no meds. It's a real joy to be back in civilization." A waiter tried to sneak past us, but I caught his attention, tripped him, actually, and ordered a couple of teas.

"How long have you been in town, J.?"

"Can't be much more than a week."

J. Edgar didn't give much thought to time on a daily basis, but he was precise in the larger sense. He always kept one eye on the night sky, and every year arrived in Amsterdam with his satchel full of antiquities exactly three days after the summer solstice. This was his one concession to the business life, a trip to Europe in the dead of summer. While the euro-youth were off doing Majorca and each other, while ameri-youth were doing Paris and London and each other, J. Edgar was squatting on the Persian carpets of the Dutch elite hustling his bones.

The tea arrived. I asked J. Edgar if he had a line on any decent smoke. This is like asking Herr Krupp if he's got a tank to sell. While Timmy Leary was still wearing a tie and writing learned papers on LSD as a possible treatment for schizoids, J. was eating peyote in Sonora. While all the college kids read *Steppenwolf* and dreamed of cocaine, J. was cutting up the Sierras of Peru with a lip full of leaf. While junkies in New York stole TV's and busted up old women to get enough fix to keep from drowning in their own snot,

J. Edgar sat in a small room in a small house on a high mountain in Kurdistan and warmed his lungs with raw opium. He was the right man to ask.

"Come on up. Got some killer bhang from Chitral."

We went to his room, which turned out to be two doors down from ours. Like ours, it had two rope beds, a ceiling fan, a small shower, but in addition he had a window. J. always got "a room with a view," even if the view was the wall of another building, even if he had to pay extra. It was a luxury he provided himself as compensation for rejecting a permanent home. He chose a permanent window instead. This particular window had a great view of the street, crammed with horse carts, motor scooter taxis, donkeys, children, hundreds of men and no women. I spotted an enormous Pashtun from the tribal areas near Afghanistan plowing through the crowd of short, nervous Pakistanis. He appeared to be just down from the hills, with bullet belts across his chest and a long rifle over his shoulder. He passed a cart piled high with goat heads and feet, tomorrow's soup, and turned into the hotel. Peshawar means "Frontier Town," and it is an apt name. You see few policemen here. They are hiding out.

J. took out his chillum, a chimney shaped ivory pipe with a stone inset for a bowl, and began to break up some hash. He took an old rag and moistened it in the sink, then wrapped it around the bottom of the pipe and handed it to me with a smile. He had been in the East long enough to know and practice the concept of ta'arof, formalized courtesy which confuses and irritates most Westerners, but does provide a way for both enemies and friends to show respect for each other. He would always pass a pipe to a guest first, always let others enter a room before him, always bow and scrape and mumble "I am your slave" to those who showed him courtesy. This often hurt his image in dealings with new clients in Amsterdam; he would appear too humble and reticent to be treated as a solid businessman. Their mistake. Trust me; this guy can bargain. He lit a match and held it to the pipe.

Four grams later, head vibrating blue green Om's of gratitude into the silent universe, I stumbled down the hall to my room. Roxy lay on her bed fanning herself and reading *"The Persian Boy."* She was wrapped in a soft yellow prayer cloth from India, her curling black hair puffed out on the pillow, her long straight nose poked deep into the book. Some bon bons and a poodle and a daytime serial are all she needs, I thought.

"Got some hash."

"Too hot to smoke," she said. She didn't look up and she didn't move. "Where'd you get it?"

"Ran into old J. Edgar down in the restaurant. Just in from Kashmir."

She sat up and began to fluff her hair with her fingers. When Roxy's in shape she's a pretty tight package, small and thin with great high tits and a butt Brazilian beach babes would envy, but we had been on vacation and on the road for five weeks. The strain of constant travel in primitive and harsh climes and the drain of one case of the shits after another had turned her gaunt and skeletal. We both looked a bit like those kids in refugee camps with scrawny little legs and gassed out bellies. Good tans, though.

"Is he coming over?" she asked.

"In a few. Then I figured we could go and check out the town. Saw some good sandals on the way in."

"Too hot. I'm going to stay right under this fan until you get us tickets out of this hole."

'Bitch,' I thought. "Fine," I said. I meant the fine part, too. Walking in a Pakistani bazaar with an unveiled Western woman is the third level of purgatory. When we were in Lahore she was grabbed and pinched and hooted at and had smoke blown in her face the entire day, and I was the one obliged to protect her. A couple of times nasty fights almost ensued; I did not have much crowd support. Overall, not a good place to be strolling with a godless foreign slut. Still, I was a bit pissed that she was copping out again. In five weeks she hadn't been out on the streets once on her own and seldom with me.

A knock, and J. Edgar shuffled in. He had put on his Pakistani disguise, white cotton pantaloons and a baggy long shirt. His short frame, angular features and 15-year tan made him look pretty local to me. Roxy jumped up and gave him a hug. A long hug.

She pulled him down beside her on the bed and held his hand. "So tell me. What have you been doing?"

I filled a chillum and handed it to J. He held it in

both hands and took a long drag through the side of his two thumbs, a technique he had learned in Kabul years back. He held the pipe out to Roxy. She pulled his hands to her mouth and took a hit and lay back on the bed. She looked like an emaciated Madonna. J. Edgar left for his room, and I took off for the market.

It was Thursday afternoon and the bazaar was crowded. Everybody in town was stocking up for the weekend. It wasn't covered like most in the East, and came complete with muddy streets and arcades which hadn't been repaired since the British left in '49. I passed a few banks; all of them had tall guards with 10 gauge shotguns sitting at the entrance. Not a town to mess around in.

I found the street with all the sandal vendors and dived in. Pakistani sandals are sturdy, two large pieces of leather crossed over at the toes and a thick strap across the back of the heels. They are reputed to last forever, though there is some doubt as to whether the sandal or your foot will break in first. Two hours later, after half a gallon of tea and long discussions of the nature of God and a sharing of my family pictures and good old bargaining, I had my sandals and headed back to the hotel.

Roxy wasn't in the room. I went to the restaurant to look for her. The usual freaks were there, but no Roxy. The Pashtun hung out at a back table and eyed the foreigners. I sat down and ordered some tea.

Half an hour later Roxy and J. Edgar came down together. Roxy was glowing. J. grabbed some tea and looked off into the distance.

"Oh, you're back. I popped over to visit J. Edgar. We had such a nice talk."

"I hope it was satisfying."

Roxy threw her head back and laughed in what she probably thought was a gay manner. All the natives in the restaurant stared at her. I could feel twelve minds simultaneously thinking "Nice Piece."

We ordered dinner and ate rather silently. Roxy tried a few more jabs, but I did the old duck and cover and didn't respond. All I really wanted was to throttle the bitch. J. Edgar ate quickly and left.

Back in the room, I stripped for bed. Roxy took another shower and lay down wet and nude on the other bed. She shined like a slick fish is the darkness.

"Want to fuck?" I asked.

"Much too hot. Check me out in the middle of the night."

No sex for three weeks, for me, at least, and I was beginning to have wet dreams for the first time since High School. Not good for the bedding. I lit a cigarette.

Roxy whispered, "I hear something in the hall."

"So?"

"Go and see."

"Probably just a rat or something."

"Go and see."

I had become accustomed to Roxy's weird flights of paranoia and figured it would be better to waste fifteen seconds on a useless trip than to argue all night; I went to the door and opened it quickly. The Pashtun from the lobby had his head against the wall.

"What in the name of God do you want?" I barked in Farsi. He smiled broadly and shrugged his shoulders, the universal sign of non-comprehension, then hurried away. I examined the wall. There were several small holes drilled in the wood. I looked through one and saw Roxy lying naked in her bed. I went back in the room and told Roxy. They must save this room for the foreign girls.

We filled the holes with pieces of paper and lay down again. No use getting in a hassle over a simple case of primitive lust. I fell asleep.

Roxy's voice woke me. She stood by the bed shivering in the heat. "He's back."

"I don't hear anything."

"Look," she said, and pointed at the wall. All the bits of paper had been poked out.

"Get back in bed."

"But then he can see me."

"If he's watching you, he won't see me."

She got in bed. I crept to the sink and filled a pitcher with water, then slid over to the door. When I stepped into the hallway, the Pashtun stood and I threw the water in his face. He ran off quickly and headed down the stairs. I went back to the room.

"That should handle it." We put the paper back in the holes and lay down again.

"Cool enough to fuck yet?"

"I'm too scared. Men can be such brutes."

"He's just doing what he's been taught. They think all Western girls are whores."

"I don't care and I don't like it."

40

"Is he wrong?"

"Fuck off." She turned over and pretended to sleep. I jumped up and grabbed her by the shoulders. "Is he wrong?"

"Leave me alone, you fucking pervert."

I was crouched over her, shook her, blood high, most blown away. My curses danced from wall to hall to roof to neighbor. When I lose it there is little hope. So. I have been like this a few times before and can assure you I am not proud. It never bought me a meal, love, admiration, nirvana, or relief. Only trouble.

I let her go and went back to my bed. Roxy pretended to cry.

I heard a noise in the hall and leapt for the door. This time, the Pashtun went up the stairs, and I took off after him. There was only one floor above us, and then the roof. The hotel was two stories higher than the next building and he couldn't jump. I attacked him, lost in it, kicking and punching and screaming epithets in Persian and English. He stood there and took it all.

Somebody pulled me off. It was J. Edgar. He yelled at the Pashtun, slapped him a couple of times and threw him to his knees. Then he took me by the arm and led me down the stairs to my room. I was shaking badly and breathing hard.

"Adrenaline rush," said J. Edgar. "You'll feel like God for the next three hours."

"Why didn't he fight back? He could have killed me easy."

"He was wrong and he knew it. If you looked at his wife, you'd be dead."

I went into the room. Roxy was snoring softly. I took a shower and went to bed, still wet.

AT PLAY IN THE FIELDS OF FERLINGHETTI

It was the best of trips, it was the worst of trips. We made it out of the San Fernando Valley before nightfall. I was concerned that my Honda 125 wouldn't carry the two of us up Interstate 5 and over the Grapevine and Tejon Pass without throwing a rod, but we took it slow and made the descent into Bakersfield just as the sun set. They made good bikes back in the '60s.

We were on the road because of an argument over the relative contributions of the Theatre of the Absurd and the Beat Generation. Ranger was of the opinion that Sam Beckett and Jean Genet had spawned Harold Pinter and Edward Albee, thus creating the most vital and vibrant literature of mid-20th Century America. I held that Burroughs and Ginsburg and Kerouac and Ferlinghetti begat Kesey and the Grateful Dead begat Bob Dylan and the Hippies and the future of all that is stoned and good in life. "Rock on, Merry Pranksters!" I cried. "Nothing to be done!" he moaned.

Ranger got his name because he once had a summer job at Sequoia National Park as a fire lookout. He was planning to be a Buddhist Vegetarian Pot Farming poet, but was majoring in business. I was planning to be dead by thirty three and changed my major every semester. By all rights, he should have been a neo-beat Gary Snyder and I should have been an existentialist corpse, but post-pubescent philosophers are not always rational and seldom become their parent's nightmares or their own dreams. He tossed a copy of Albee's "Who's

Afraid of Virginia Woolf?" at my head; I slapped Ginsberg's "Howl" into his burgeoning beer paunch; we squatted at opposite corners of our dorm room and sulked.

His sulking turned to enrapt reading. The angel headed hipsters were getting to him, I could tell. It was time to administer the coup de grace, force him to admit my superior insight and wisdom, but the doubly depressing Ms. Woolf and Mr. Albee were not helping. My mind was a cacophony of wimpy professors and bitch academic wives. Fortuitously, Ranger provided me the blade for his own gutting.

"I admit it; some of this stuff is OK. But if these beatniks are so good, how come they can't find a bigger and better publisher than City Lights?"

I went off on the obscenity trial over "Howl," the judicial establishment of "redeeming social importance" as a result, the range and fame of the many writers City Lights had brought to print.

"Prove it," he snickered.

"Let us go there, you and I," I cried.

And we set off for San Francisco through the etherized Long Beach dusk to visit the publisher of my dreams.

By the time we hit Los Banos, it was midnight and the moon was rising. The night had turned chill, and we were unprepared. Ranger developed a severe case of the shivers, and I was afraid he would wobble the bike into oncoming truck traffic, so we stopped at a roadside gas and guzzle station for coffee. Someone had left a copy of the New York Times on our table.

Ranger got a gleam in his eye, grabbed the paper, and headed for the bathroom. When he returned, he looked a bit like an Iowa scarecrow, with scraps of newspaper showing through his jacket sleeves and collar and pant legs. He had stuffed the newsprint in and around himself as insulation against the cold. Despite my distain for his debauched academic ideals, I, too, had felt the frigid fingers of the night, and recognized the wisdom of his innovation. I took to the restroom to caulk my own clothing.

It was a piercing Siberian cold as we putted up Pacheco Pass, but the newsprint saved our skinny college boy carcasses from hypothermal death. We could smell Gilroy as we came out of the hills. Garlic Capital of the World. Not so swell at 3:00 am on a foggy icebox Spring morning. We fled north toward San Francisco as fast as the Honda would take us and arrived at the southern city limits as the sun rose, around six. We went straight to the City Lights Bookstore, but it didn't open until ten, so we parked the motorcycle and strolled over to the recently opened Condor Club, America's first topless bar, to stare at Carol Doda's fabulous breasts as depicted on the neon sign out front, then down to Chinatown for some Dim Sum and black tea. By the time we finished drooling and dining, the bookstore was open.

We cockwalked in with schoolboy swagger, and there, at the cash register, was the satyr himself, the bearded balding half god half man who had found a way to monetize verse, to support himself off the rantings of drug deranged beatniks, the Lawrence of

Ferlinghetti himself. My backbone, confidence, and cool all disappeared and I bolted for the basement, where the poetry books lived, Ranger on my heels.

"That's him, right?"

"Yeah."

"Well, here's your chance to talk to your hero."

"I can't."

"Why not?"

"I can't."

"Fucking coward. I'd talk to Albee if he were here."

"Easy to say, hard to do."

"Fucking coward."

Ranger was pissing me off, but the blood began to flow again. I wandered through the stacks, grabbing books by Gregory Corso, William Burroughs, Paul Bowles, and yes, Lawrence Ferlinghetti.

"Come on," I said to Ranger. "I'm going up."

The Man had on a floppy fedora and was reading a play. I think it was "Waiting for Godot." I put my books down, and as Ferlinghetti started to ring them up, my mouth began to run.

"Hey, man, we just drove up from Long Beach on a motorcycle through the night and the mountains and the garlic of Gilroy just to see you and the bookstore and the holy font of all that is good and right about life and literature and we get here and lookit here you you you are right where I pictured you and...."

"That'll be seven bucks."

"Cool, that's cool. Here you go, man. Hey, do you

46

know how much you mean…"

"Fuck off, kid."

He pulled the hat brim low over his forehead and went back to reading. Ranger and I slunk out of the bookstore and fired up the bike.

"At least he spoke to you," Ranger said.

We wove through traffic and headed for Highway One. Might as well take a new route home.

GONE FISHING
Goa Coast, 1973

Rajiv led the way over the lava outcropping just as the sun was rising. His feet were bare, but two inches of callous protected them from the razor sharp rocks. My snazzy running shoes were hacked and ragged already, and I was afraid they wouldn't make it back to the hut. As we topped a small volcanic hill, the Arabian Sea opened, rimmed with tall palms and rice paddies and café au lait beaches. We were on a cliff fifteen feet above a protected bay eaten into the rocky part of the shoreline with fishing on our minds.

I had been warned not to expect much. It was the off season. The fish had gone to happier places, and only crabs were hanging around. The rains came blasting down twice each day, once in late morning and again in the early evening. Even the hippies had left Goa for Nepal and Kashmir and any other place the summer monsoon might miss or only kiss in passing. Good thing. I was sick of hippies after two months on the road.

Rajiv's pole was a nine foot switch of bamboo with a metal grommet screwed into the tip. He ran a strand of 50 pound monofil through the eyelet. One end was wrapped around a stick that served as his reel. He tied a desiccated chicken back to the other end and dropped it into the churning water below, unraveling the line to let it sink to the bottom. We sat on the rocks and waited in silence.

Rajiv was good at silence. In the month I had been staying in the guest room he built on the side of his

49

hut for Silk Road wanderers like me, he had spoken perhaps five hundred words. He lived in a jungle area a half mile from the beach, and though there were neighbors only thirty meters away, you couldn't see their shacks through the random tangle of banana and papaya trees that grew in clumps around and between the two rice paddies that provided enough sustenance to keep him from migrating to a life of poverty in the city. There was no electricity or phone line or connection to the outside world except his feet. In the evenings, he and his wife would sit in the kitchen while the rains poured down and stare at the wall while I ate the rice and vegetable curry they had prepared for my dinner. When I thanked them and left for my room to read or write for a while by candle light, they would nod me adieu and turn their eyes back to the barren wall.

Rajiv felt something tug at the line and slowly wound the monofil around his stick as he drew his bait out of the sea. Two small crabs, perhaps six inches across the back, were clinging to the chicken. He gently raised them to our perch above the bay and knocked them off into a burlap rice bag he had brought to hold his catch. The chicken still had some flesh on it, so he dropped it back into the water.

I had come fishing with Rajiv for two reasons. First, I had to get out of my room for the day. His wife Bharat was doing her weekly resurfacing of my walls and floor. She had bought several kilos of dried water buffalo dung from what she referred to as a rich neighbor. While I moved my sleeping bag and backpack gear to the kitchen, she mixed up the buff dung with some water in a large clay vessel. She plastered the entire room with the fetid mess, about a quarter inch thick. It took several hours to dry, and left a seamless, soft, and mildly odiferous surface that was pleasant to the touch and gentle on a sleeper's back.

My second reason was more selfish. I am a man who fishes. I had brought hooks and a few spoons and spinners and flies on my journey in hopes that I might try my luck trout fishing in Chitral or tie into a giant Golden Mahseer in the Rampaganga River as it raced down from the foothills of the Himalayas. So far, my efforts had ended in futility; Waziri tribesmen had blown up the road to Chitral in anger at some Pakistani politician's plan to create a summer resort in the area, and I had been busted at the Rampaganga by an overzealous policeman who insisted I needed a fishing license. He could get me one for a mere $100. Years ago, when I began my journeys in the East, I took a solemn vow to never grease the palm of a corrupt provincial official, so I left in a huff, my dream of a fifty inch fighting Mahseer on the line dashed forever. Besides, $100 could carry me for almost a month in this part of the world.

Rajiv pulled up a half dozen crabs in the first hour. I watched the flow of the water as it rushed into the small bay, climbed down the rocks and felt its temperature, gathered some scallops growing in a tide pool on the adjacent beach. In similar areas on the coast of Mexico, under similar weather and tidal conditions, fish would never gather at the bottom, where the water was churned up by the in and out flow of the sea. They would be up a ways, where the territory was calmer. I asked Rajiv if I could try my hand.

I cut the chicken off the line, tied on a hook, and baited it with bit of scallop flesh. I dropped the rig to the bottom, then lifted it about eight feet. Two minutes later I got a strike and pulled out an eighteen incher that looked similar to a mackerel. Rajiv seemed stunned. He spoke for the first time since breakfast. "Not possible. No fish this time of year."

I rebaited the hook, dropped it in, and bam...two minutes and another mack. I baited up again and handed the rod to Rajiv...three minutes and wham...another mack. In an hour we had a dozen fish and the rice bag was full.

We headed down the hill and followed a path two miles through the jungle to Arpoa, the nearest village with a market that day. There were maybe fifteen stalls selling rice and phosphate fertilizer and plastic sandals and tin pots. One old lady had bananas and coconuts. Another had needles and thread. When Rajiv opened his bag and pulled out a fish, the market folks went quiet, then crazy. They gathered around us, flapping like starving chickens at a feeding station. Everyone wanted a fish. We traded one for a kilo of rice, another for two pair of sandals. One grandmother brought us twelve yards of sari cloth in exchange for three fish. We kept one mackerel for dinner and made it back to the hut just before the rains came. The water buff crap in my room was dry, and I got my gear back in as the deluge hit.

Bharat was ecstatic. It was a rare thing for her to receive presents from her husband. They lived in a barter economy, and the rent that I and other nomads paid them while drifting through the Orient usually went for necessities like charcoal or fertilizer. I thought her favorite would be the sari cloth, but it was the needles and thread that made her cry. She held them in one hand and stroked Rajiv's cheek with the other while she offered thanks. It was the first time I had seen her touch him in the month I had been staying there.

That night, Bharat cooked up a curry with the fish. Back home, it would have been enough flesh to feed three, possibly four, but here in rural Goa it is different. She invited more neighbors than I knew she had, about fourteen people, to share in the feast. All of us sat around the tiny kitchen staring at the walls and forming balls of curry and rice with the fingers of our right hands and popping them in our mouths. Rajiv seemed pleased that he could share his bounty. After the neighbors left, I asked him if there was anything in the world that would make him a happier man. "A water buffalo," he smiled. "Then my life would be perfect."

The next morning broke bright and sunny. I asked Rajiv if we could fish again. I had a hidden agenda; I figured if he was the only local dude who knew how to catch fish in the summertime, he could set up a stall in the market, save up some money, and buy his own water buffalo. I calculated it would take about $500, and maybe two summers of fishing could bring that in. He was already knee deep in one of his rice paddies when I asked, but he washed the mud off his hands and grabbed the pole.

When we got to the bay by the beach, I offered Rajiv a hook. He shook his head, took a piece of desiccated chicken from his rice bag and tied it to the monofil.

THE RIVER

Eddie had to look after Gramps until Mom got home, and he was not happy. He had to skip soccer practice at the High School, and babysitting the old man was never any fun. Last week, Gramps found the gun Mom hid and threatened to kill himself, but he couldn't find the bullets. When he was in a mood he was hard to control. Even at 80, Gramps was sturdy.

Eddie heard the front door slam. Gramps was on the loose, in the wild. Eddie ran out to the porch and saw him heading straight for the river. He overtook Gramps twenty feet short of the bank and grabbed his arm.

"Where you goin', Gramps?"

"Who the hell are you?"

"Eddie, Gramps. Come on back to the house."

"I got business." Gramps tore his arm away and ran for the water.

Eddie caught him at the riverbank and wrestled him to the ground. The old man was still farm strong, and it was tough to keep him down. Finally, he stopped struggling.

They both stood up and brushed the sand and mud from their clothes. Gramps put his hand on Eddie's shoulder and looked him in the eye. "Eddie, you got to let me do it. I'm worthless to anyone. You got to let me."

"You called me Eddie."

"What's that?

"You called me Eddie."

"Who's Eddie?"

They walked back to the house. Gramps sat on the porch while Eddie made coffee. Gramps liked it hot and black.

THE FISHER GIRLS

Chapter 1: The Idea

Four cousins were trying to have fun one day, but they had played with all the games in the house and were tired of them. They had watched all the cartoons on the TV and were tired of watching. They were bored.

Eva was the oldest, so she called her cousins together. Camille, Alexa and Marina sat around her in the back yard. "There's nothing to do." Eva said. "Does anybody have an idea of what would be fun?"

Camille said, "Let's go to the playground and find some boys to play with."

Alexa said, "I'm thirsty and want some milk, but there's no milk in the refrigerator."

Marina said, "I'm hungry. I want to eat."

Eva said, ' Can't you guys agree? You seem to want everything in the world."

Marina, who was the youngest, yelled, "I want to eat. I want to eat. I want to eat a fish fillet."

Alexa said, "Stop screaming. Where are we going to find a fish? We don't have any money, and there are no fish in the refrigerator."

Camille said, "Maybe we can go fishing."

Well. The other girls looked at each other. They all shouted at once, "That's a great idea. Let's go fishing."

Chapter 2: Getting Ready

Now the girls had a problem. They wanted to go fishing, but they didn't have anything to go fishing with. They had no fishing rods and they had no string to tie to the rods and they had no hooks to tie to the strings.

Eva said, "I know where we can get fishing rods. We can get them in the woods behind the house."

So the four cousins walked out through the backyard gate into the woods beyond the garden. They found old, thin tree branches lying on the ground. Some of them were crooked, so they wouldn't make good fishing rods, but some of them were straight. The girls took the straightest ones to use for their fishing rods. But they still needed some string.

Camille said, "Look. There's a vine growing on that tree. It looks pretty strong. We could make our fishing line from the vines."

So the four girls collected some vines that were growing on the trees, and tied them to the fishing rods. But they still needed hooks.

Alexa said, "I know what we can use for hooks. Come with me."

She led all the girls out of the woods and through the backyard and back into the house and up to her room. She pulled a beautiful box made of wood and satin out from under her bed. Inside the box were all the treasures she had been saving. She liked pretty rocks and birthday cards and magic rings. But one of her favorite things to save was wishbones from the delicious turkeys that her grandmother cooked. She had four of them in her special box. Grandmother said that wishbones were magic. If you made a wish, and you and a friend broke the wishbone, and you had the biggest piece of it in your hand, your wish would come true. And even better—the big part of the wishbone looked just like a hook.

So Eva and Camille took the first wishbone and they pulled on it and it broke and Camille had the biggest part. She was sure she would get her wish. And even better–she had a hook to tie to the string on her fishing rod.

Eva and Alexa took the second wishbone and they pulled on it and it broke and Alexa had the biggest part. She was sure she would get her wish. And even better–she had a hook to tie to the string on her fishing rod.

Eva and Marina took the third wishbone and they pulled on it and it broke and Marina had the biggest part. She was sure she would get her wish. And even better–she had a hook to tie to the string on her fishing rod.

Eva just couldn't seem to win. She could have been mad or she could have been sad or she could have even been bad. But instead, she took the fourth wishbone and held one part in her left hand

and one part in her right hand and pulled. She had the big piece she needed for her hook, and she put the small piece in her pocket.

Now all the girls were ready to go fishing.

Chapter 3: The Fish

The four cousins walked out of the house and across the backyard and into the woods. After a few minutes, they came to a beautiful little river with trees hanging over its banks and birds singing in the trees and butterflies flying over the water. The sun was bright and the sky was blue and it was a perfect day to go fishing.

The four friends all used their new fishing rods to throw their wishbone hooks out into the river. Then they sat on the riverbank and waited for the fish to bite their hooks.

And waited.

And waited.

And waited.

They all pulled in their hooks. There were no fish on the hooks.

Eva said, "This is not going well."

Camille said, "I wish one of us really knew how to fish."

Alexa said, "I'm thirsty."

And Marina said, "There's no food on this hook to make the fish want to eat it."

And all the other girls shouted, "She's right. Marina's right."

Eva said, "I wonder what a fish would like to eat?"

Camille said, "Probably not what we like to eat."

Alexa said, "I'm thirsty."

And Marina said, "They like to eat worms."

All the other girls shouted, "Worms. They're slimy and squiggly and squirmy. I wouldn't ever eat a worm."

Marina said, "You're not a fish."

And Marina turned around and started digging in the ground and found a worm. She took it back to the river and tied it on to her wishbone hook and threw it way out into the middle of the river.

And she waited.

And waited.

And waited.

And just when she was starting to think that the worm wasn't such a good idea, something pulled very hard on her worm and wishbone bait and almost pulled the fishing rod out of her hands.

But Marina fought hard to hold on to the fishing rod, and pulled and pulled and pulled. And finally she pulled a big, big fish from the river.

That fish was almost as big as Marina. It was mostly silver, but the sides of its body flashed like a rainbow in the sun. Marina had caught a fish to eat.

But the fish was so beautiful, and it was having a hard time breathing as it lay on the rocks beside the river.

Marina said, "I wished for a fish and I caught one, but I love this fish. I think it wants to be at home with its family. I'm going to put her back in the water."

And she did.

Marina was still hungry, but she felt really good anyway.

Alexa said, "I'm thirsty."

Chapter 4: The Cow

The other girls thought that when Marina set the beautiful fish free, it was a wonderful thing to do, but they were maybe a little jealous because she had caught something but they had not.

Alexa said, "Marina caught a fish with a worm. Maybe if I try a different bait, I'll catch something different."

Alexa looked around and tried to guess what might make a good bait. The leaves in the trees were too high for her to reach, and the mushrooms she found growing were too icky, and the bark on the trees was too hard. She sat down in the grass to think. She felt the grass. It felt really nice.

Alexa said, "I'll use this grass for my bait."

The other girls thought this was silly, but Alexa tied a bunch of grass to her wishbone fish hook and threw her wishbone bait far out into the middle of the river.

And she waited.

And waited.

And waited.

And just when she was starting to think that the grass wasn't such a good idea, something pulled very hard on her grass and wishbone bait and almost pulled the fishing rod out of her hands.

But Alexa fought hard to hold on to the fishing rod, and pulled and pulled and pulled. And finally she pulled a huge cow from the river.

That cow was twice as big as Alexa. It was mostly brown, but the sides of its body had big round white spots. The cow must have been a mommy, because her udder was full of milk. Alexa had caught a cow that she could milk. She could drink the milk, and then she wouldn't be thirsty.

But the cow looked so sad. It was probably thinking about her little baby calf, who was probably lost and hungry and probably needed her mother to feed her.

Alexa said, "I wished for something to drink, and I caught a cow that could give me milk, but I love this cow. I think it wants to be at home with its family. I'm going to let her go free and find her baby.

And she did.

Alexa was still thirsty, but she felt really good anyway.

Camille said, "I'm bored. Let's go to the park and find some boys to play with."

Chapter 5: The Boy

The other girls thought that Camille was just bored because she hadn't caught something yet. They told her to stop thinking about boys and to start thinking about what kind of bait she would use if she wanted to get her wish.

Camille looked around and tried to guess what might make a good bait. The pinecones in the trees were too high for her to reach, and the fiddle head ferns were too pretty to pick, and the dandelions blew away every time she picked one. She sat down by the river to think. And then she saw a piece of paper floating in the water, right near the shore. She reached out and grabbed it.

It was a birthday card that somebody lost. Right in the center of the birthday card was a heart.

Camille said, "I'll use this heart for my bait."

The other girls thought this was silly, but Camille carefully tied the paper heart to her wishbone fish hook and threw her wishbone bait far out into the middle of the river.

And she waited.

And waited.

And waited.

And just when she was starting to think that the paper heart wasn't such a good idea, something pulled very hard on her heart and wishbone bait and almost pulled the fishing rod out of her hands.

But Camille fought hard to hold on to the fishing rod, and pulled and pulled and pulled. And finally she pulled a very small boy from the river.

That boy was twice as small as Camille. He was really cute and had curly brown hair. Camille finally had a boy she could play with.

She tried to give him a hug, but he ran behind a tree and cried, "I want my mommy!"

Camille said, "I wished for a boy to play with, and I caught one. But I love this boy. I think he wants to be at home with its family. I wish I could find them."

Just then, the four friends heard a terrible scream. It sounded like, "Charlie.... Charlie..... Where are you?"

"Over here. Over here," yelled Camille. "I found your little boy."

A very scared Mommy and Daddy ran out of the woods and down to the river and picked up their little boy and hugged him and kissed him. And then they picked up Camille and hugged her and kissed her and thanked her for saving Charlie's life. He had fallen in the river, and Camille had fished him out.

Camille didn't have a boy to play with, but she felt really good anyway.

Eva said, "Marina catches a fish with a worm. Alexa catches a cow with grass. Camille catches a boy with her heart. What the heck is going on here?"

Chapter 6: The Basket

The other girls thought that Eva asked way too many questions. She always wanted to know how things worked and why they worked and what they were really like. The cousins told her to stop asking why this and what that and to start thinking about what kind of bait she would use to get her wish.

Eva looked around and tried to guess what might make a good bait. The tiger lilies were too pretty to pick, and the blueberries she found growing were not ripe, and the milkweed pods were way too hard. She sat down by herself in a little clearing under a pine tree and looked at the mountains. She thought about the world and all the people, some happy and some sad, and how it would be wonderful if she could help make the world a nicer place for everyone.

Eva said, "Oh well. I guess there'll be plenty of time to save the world when I grow up."

And then she had an idea. Lots of needles had fallen from the pine tree. She gathered them up and wove a basket out of the pine needles. The basket was small and round and very strong.

Eva said, "I'll use this basket for my bait."

The other girls thought this was silly, but Eva carefully tied the pine needle basket to her wishbone fish hook and threw her wishbone bait far out into the middle of the river.

And she waited.

And waited.

And waited.

And just when she was starting to think that the pine needle basket wasn't such a good idea, something pulled very hard on her basket and wishbone bait and almost pulled the fishing rod out of her hands.

But Eva fought hard to hold on to the fishing rod, and pulled and pulled and pulled. And finally she pulled the basket from the river. At first, it seemed like the basket was just the same as when she cast it into the water, but then Eva looked inside.

There was a whole little world in that basket. There were little mountains and little trees and little fields of fruit and grain. There were tiny farmhouses and tiny villages and tiny big cities. There were lots of little people and cat and dogs. And Eva thought she saw a happy rainbow colored fish swimming in a river, and a smiling cow feeding her baby calf, and a little boy playing in his backyard.

That world was as small as anything Eva had ever seen. It was peaceful and safe, and everyone seemed to be so happy. Eva finally had a beautiful world that was all her own.

She smiled and looked at her small world again, but something was wrong.

Water was dripping out of a hole in the

basket. The land that the small people were using to grow their crops was turning dry. The trees and plants were turning brown and shriveling up. The cities and villages and farmhouses were starting to crumble and turn to dust. The small people were crying and confused and didn't know what was happening to their world.

But Eva knew. She had taken the beautiful small world away from where it should be, and it was losing all the water it needed to live. Eva didn't know what to do. She put her hands in her pockets and scrunched up her shoulders, because that's what she did sometimes when she was thinking very hard. And in her pocket she found the small piece of wishbone she had broken off before. It was just the perfect size to fill up the hole in her basket world.

She took the basket off her magic fish hook and put the small, broken piece of wishbone in the hole. She cupped her hands and took some water from the river and sprinkled it over the little basket world. All the little people came out and danced for joy in the rain. Eva placed the basket gently back in the river. As the little basket world floated away, Eva thought she could hear a million small voices whispering, "Thank you, my friend."

Eva didn't have a world that was all her own, but she felt really good anyway.

And the four fisher girls all held hands and walked home to their own back yard.

TRAVELS WITH CHARLES
By
Pinchy Perra
(as told to C.E. Watts)

The snow started just east of the Santiam Pass. Charles, my Sapien companion, had to drive. My race is cursed with the lack of an opposable thumb, and I can only steer on roads with no curves. Besides, my legs are too short to reach the pedals. All I could do was watch and pray as he slid our overstuffed Subaru up the mush covered mountain road. The truck in front of us had even more trouble, especially in the curves, and at one point smacked into a guard rail and almost lost its load into the canyon below. I almost lost my load watching.

I was glad to leave Oregon. Two weeks with that crazy princess of a Shih Tzu that cohabits with my Sapien's brother was quite enough, thank you. I don't like those pure bred lap breeds. They think they own the couch, and don't even bother to kick dirt on their own poop. Whatever. We half breeds live longer, run faster, and catch more Frisbees. When I heard we were heading back home to the Adirondacks, I rolled in the grass like a puppy for an hour, filled with gratitude.

Charles passed the truck when it pulled over to put on chains and continued to drive maniacally up the highway. He kept saying, "Come on, come on, come on. We can beat this thing." He's not very articulate, but I think he meant we were going to race the storm over the crest of the mountain. I knew the car had bald tires and didn't recall any chains being packed, so I figured we were either dead meat or soon to be stuck in some snow bank. Out of my paws. I took a nap.

When I awoke, we were in eastern Oregon and the sky had cleared. I tried to stretch, but that was quite a trick, given the space Charles had provided me in the cramped and over packed car. He thinks a two by three piece of foam covered with a crappy Mexican tourist blanket is space enough for a mid size Canine. Does he not watch me run for hours on the Northville trail when summer is at its peak? Does he seriously think I will be pleasant to him when all I get for exercise for the next week is the occasional piddle stop at some State run rest area? A ten minute walk on a leash? Oppression is what I call it, pure and simple.

I dozed off again and woke when the car stopped. That usually means we get gas, we "walk on a leash," or we stop for the night. The hotel sign was missing a letter, but I think it said "Bates otel." A nice young man checked us in and invited us to dinner with his mom, but we were tired and politely declined. The shower dripped all night. I, for one, slept fitfully. In the morning the old lady herself checked us out. She was a dead copy of her son. I suspect inbreeding.

I was excited about the chance to cross Wyoming; I'd heard tales of short little deer with tiny antlers. I asked Charles what they were called over a month ago, but Sapiens are remarkably slow in responding to mind messages. I have to repeat myself over and over and over (he calls it "barking") and it can be months before he gives me an answer. Anyway, he finally told me they are "antelope." What a cool name. I rolled it around in my throat for awhile, just because it felt so good, but Charles told me to stop whining. I ignored him.

It was two hours before he pulled into a rest area. In my world, that is abuse. Am I supposed to wet my bedding because he wants to drive an extra 20 minutes or forgets to take me out when he refills his coffee? And then he pulls out without stopping. I got so mad I was about to piss on his dirty shirts when he turned off on some country road and opened the door. No leash! Freedom! I ran flat out for twenty minutes and I needed every one. It turns out the rest area didn't allow Canines. This is discrimination most foul, and I intend to have my Sapien write our congresswoman as soon as we get to Lake Placid. There should be a law. Charles and I discussed it and decided to use isolated country roads as our rest stops for the remainder of the trip.

It was 400 miles to the border with Nebraska, and we didn't see a single antelope. Sam and Daisy, my neighbors in New York, had specifically asked for an eye witness description of the legendary beast. I moped for an hour about my failure. Charles asked if something was wrong, but I ignored him. We slept in some dump of a Motel 6 in the middle of nowhere. It smelled of so many random Canines that I couldn't get a grip on who had been there or when or even how many. It is my duty to know such things. The cacophony of scents gave me a migraine. I took a dog biscuit and crashed.

By ten the next morning we were in Iowa and the land began to change. The earth was dark and smelled of manure and feral Canines. I knew there were fox and coyotes in the territory, and I am convinced I caught the whiff of a real wolf, my race's god and godfather. I saw a coyote once, but never a wolf. Now that would be a story for Sam and Daisy.

The wind was howling (I love that word) and Charles decided to close the windows. What a strange and thoughtless race these Sapiens are. Am I supposed to subsist on the odors of the car? The same old ones I've been snuffing for three days? Where is the adventure in that? I start to grumble, and for once Charles gets the message. He opens the window to let me breathe, and a dirty shirt he forgot to pack securely blew out of the back and over his head. He swerved into the line of oncoming traffic and clawed at the shirt, totally blind. He finally ripped it off and just avoided an eighteen wheeler as he jerked the Subaru back into our lane. What a putz.

Why do we stay with these creatures? They speak to us in baby talk, feed us when they want and not when we're hungry, leave us alone for hours at a time. I have never understood the Canine need to live with companion animals, but I must admit I feel better when they are around. Sapiens are not bright, but they are very accepting of the love we Canines are born with and must give away to be happy. And they give great massages.

We stopped for the night in a place called Davenport. I could smell a great river nearby. The flat lands were behind us and the wind blowing from the east brought a hint of mountains to come. I tried to tell Charles of my excitement, but he growled at me and rolled over in his bed. If he wants to be grumpy, that's his privilege; I don't have to buy into it. I dreamt of antelope on the high Plains.

The next day started average and quickly deteriorated. We crossed a broad river, but were going so fast I couldn't read the sign on the bridge. It said something like "Missus Sippi." Must be named after an Italian woman. The first few hours were ok, but then the smells began to change. I knew a city was coming, and I suppose it's time to admit that I hate cities. Canines who have lived there and escaped to the country can seldom talk about the experience unless they have had counseling. They tell of being locked in concrete towers with only a box of sand to defecate in, of "dog parks" filled with repressed and aggressive Canines driven mad by the isolation and artificiality of such an empty life. Charles seemed agitated too. He began to cough and water started to ooze from his eyes. He pulled over and looked at a map. Soon we were in the country again. I smelled raccoons. Bliss. I fell asleep.

I had nightmares about the city. Stone monoliths with myriad golden eyes and covered with soot rose above narrow streets crowded with cars, many of them yellow, belching foul gases and blaring something Charles calls music. Sapiens were everywhere, and I was one of the poor leashed Canines being dragged along the street. I dreamed I escaped and made a run for the park, but a large man in a blue suit was chasing me with a butterfly net. I woke with a start, happy it was just a dream, then noticed we were on a mighty bridge over a mighty river. The sign said "Hudson." To my horror, I realized we were entering a metropolis with buildings as high as the clouds and more cars than I could chase in a lifetime. So this was hell.

Charles went crazy. He swerved in and out of traffic, barely missing double parked cars, screaming and slamming on the brakes and swearing out the window like a Doberman on a raw meat high. We cut across the bow of one of the yellow cars and bounced into a cave under one of the concrete mountains. Some Sapien with a Weimaraner joined us; we leashed up and headed for the streets. The Weimaraner was cool. He actually liked the city. He said there was a sense of order. He awoke when his Sapien awoke. They went to the same park twice a day, always at the same time. He ate twice a day, two cups of canned goop he had learned to like. He was upbeat, but I pitied him.

He was right about the park, though. It was chilly and green and almost like the real country. If that's all you knew, I guess you could find a reasonable quality of life in such a place. I, however, have seen the larger world and wouldn't live here for a truckload of desiccated steak.

We left early in the morning. All the cars had

disappeared; I presume they went to sleep in caves like the one where our Subaru spent the night. As we drove, the hills grew larger and the air more pure. I actually thought I could smell the hemlocks that grow beside our house. I dozed off into the most peaceful sleep of the last five days.

Frantic barking snapped me into consciousness. I looked out the window and saw Sam and Daisy jumping at the car, all slobbery mouthed and sentimental about my return. Charles opened the door and I leapt out. It's a bit embarrassing to admit. but I lost my typical sophisticated aloofness and joined my friends in a rough and carefree romp around the yard, all fake snarls and flying chest bumps. Hurricane and Rosy, who live up the hill, heard the ruckus and raced down to join us. It felt great to be back in the pack. Eventually, they all went home for dinner, but not before making plans for the morrow. Exhausted, I laid down under my favorite pine tree in the front yard. Man, it's good to be home. My Sapien seems happy too.

BROKEN GLASS

Three a.m. and it's the cops again. My Cubans are down at the agency smashing up our sorry fleet of used Chevys and Fords with two by fours. Get my ass down there.

My Cubans hate me. The Refugee agency down the street puts their Cubans on welfare and in public housing and on food stamps. They give them all the time they want to learn English and lots of warm and fuzzy social services talk on how to be good citizens. I make my Cubanos work. Most of them are lazy ingrates and criminals used to getting everything free from a tropical island paradise dedicated to socialist lassitude. Nobody had to labor in order to eat or screw or party. Pick a banana, drink some rum, rob a tourist; all was provided. They like to sing and dance and get drunk and fight. They like to intimidate people. Thus the smashing of the agency armada. My Cubans are showing me they care.

Emily gets them the jobs, actually, but I'm her boss at the moment, so I take the heat. Emily is a wonder. Big bottle red hair and remnants of a New Orleans accent. Big red lips and a lust for yours truly. Or anyone. She is a needy woman. She wants to replace me as head of the agency.

She is the best job developer I ever saw. Most of our refugees have poor language skills at best, and their working habits seem bizarre to American bosses. For example, all of them need a nap at midday; that really pisses off the gringos. The circadian clock of the USA is wound so tight that there is no room for real leisure or moments of peace, only vacations more frantic than work and round after round of gym and golf and soccer for the kids. Never has there been a nation more sleep deprived. Emily uses this as a tool to pry open minimum wage opportunities for our people. When she is talking to some droopy eyed personnel dweeb about some trash hauling gig and the dweeb says "but they don't speak English," Emily asks if the garbage speaks English. They have no defense against her. It helps that she shops at upscale resale outlets and dresses like a neurotic hotel heiress, all stiletto heels and tight designer suits that scream power and highlight her love handles. Emily intimidates.

She was already at the office when I arrived. The cops were off on one side of the parking lot, smoking and bitching about all the trouble we caused by bringing these foreign losers into their community. Emily had the Cubans sitting on the steps of our dumpy refugee resettlement office. She was lecturing them.

"What the hell you boys doin' smashin' up our cars? These are your cars too, you know. Who you think you're dealin' with here?"

She tried screaming, on the assumption that if she made the message louder they would instantaneously learn the language. They didn't understand a word, but got the message anyway: Miss Emmy was pissed, and they better chill. Juan, the only one who had

80

learned any English at all, tried to make peace. He was the leader of the Cuban gang, and he was in love with Emily; she was heavy and liked to hug young muscular black men. She reminded him of home.

"We fix the cars, you not worry."

I knew he was right. Cubans are masters of chicken wire and body putty. When I first got here, the thief running the agency at the time had a couple of 15 passenger vans with computer chips for brains. If they broke, you had to take them to the shop. The shop was owned by his son-in-law. Beaucoup bucks When I got rid of him, I dumped the trucks and bought a bunch of beater cars for $500 apiece. Every refugee in the world is an auto mechanic, so no more maintenance costs. We saved enough to build a community kitchen in the basement. In all things there is a balance. We'd have to pay for the windshields and glass, but I could take that out of their monthly stipends from the home office and they'd still have enough for cigars and rum. I talked to the police. They wanted to "throw their sorry criminal asses" into the local jail; I refused to press charges. Juan would kill me for sure.

These guys were Santeria, a voodoo-like sect that criminals in Castro's jails took up to enhance the pain of their lives in prison. Gangster theology. Tattoos were considered rites of passage. Lots of these Cubanos had tats on their lips and tongues; Juan had black scorpions with red stingers on the inside of his eyelids. The others respected him. Me too.

When the boatlift of refugees began pouring out

of Cuba in '80, Havana flushed its jails and insane asylums into the stream. About 10% of the refugees coming out of the port of Mariel were the criminal dregs of socialist society. Castro called them gusanos, worms, and cast them onto the shores of America. Go forth and find your freedom, scum. Most went to Miami, but not all. Our gusanos found their liberty in the Silicon Valley.

By the time Mrs. Nguyen arrived at seven, her regular time, the gray base paint was already drying on the busted cars. Mrs. Nguyen is in charge of the Vietnamese and other assorted South East Asian refugees we bring in, so nobody bothered to call her about the Cubans. She is prim and proper and tiny and always has a smile. She speaks five languages and has a degree in French Literature from the Sorbonne. She got home from Paris just as the Viet Cong were conquering Saigon. Her father was Education Minister in the defeated government, and the family decided to flee. The boat her family used to smuggle them out of the country was attacked by Thai pirates in the South China Sea and she was raped uncountable times; her father and brothers were killed trying to protect her. The pirates put sand in the boat's engine and left them, naked and powerless, to the monsoon winds. When the boat drifted into the harbor at Kuala Terengganu, it got spun around by the breakwater and capsized. Her mother and seven sisters and fiancé and all her aunts and uncles and cousins to the third degree drowned in the pounding surf. 187 dead. I saw her records from the refugee camp in Malaysia; she was twenty three and the only survivor. She never married, but calls herself Mrs. She has never talked about any of it. I am thinking of making her my replacement.

The New York office wants me out of here. The Soviets just invaded Afghanistan and a couple of million refugees have inundated Pakistan. I want to be there, where the action is, but am obliged to finish up this lame assignment here in San Jose, a truly loathsome and isolated place. You walk down the street and nobody's there. You have to go to a strip mall to find people, and they are... they are not worth finding. Mostly the trophy wives of potbellied men with large misshapen heads and pocket protectors. the Aliens who run our arrogant new world. Give me Peshawar anytime.

I came here to fire the former Director. He stole eighty thousand in government resettlement funds and spent it all on his granddaughters; not even a sweater for himself. Everybody loved and respected him as an icon of the local humanitarian community. Twenty five years of honorable service to the dispossessed of the world, and then his kid has a kid. And another one. And he can't do enough for the little princesses on his pitiful non-profit salary, and it's his time or whatever he tells himself. Nobody will notice. When I confronted him and the Board of Directors with our audit, he denied everything. The Board was a bunch of clueless do-gooders handpicked for gullibility, socialites looking for letterhead material. He's out of work and on his way to jail. I ditched the Directors for their blatant failure to even glance at the books, disbanded the non-profit they used to funnel in our resettlement money from the government, recruited a new Board made up of community organizers and leftist accountants, and incorporated a replacement agency. Axe man work. Sometimes fun, usually not. It is done. Now I have to choose someone to run the damn thing so I can beat a dance out of this hole. It's down to Emily and Mrs. Nguyen.

The Vietnamese are conservative family folk, and they don't like Emily. She dresses like an off duty pole dancer, dips her face in lakes of paint and powder, laughs way too loud and way too often. The Cubans don't care much for Mrs. Nguyen. They find her formal and cold. She'll smile and interact, but there is always a distance. She never physically touches them. She never touches anyone.

The police call again around noon. Some indefinable problem with a class full of Vietnamese kids at the middle school in Palo Alto. Get my ass up there.

I grab Mrs. Nguyen and we head for the school. Cop cars littered the parking lot and the ambulances were just arriving. Some son-of-a-nouveau-riche-computer millionaire had tossed a cherry bomb into an English language class full of refugee kids. They thought it was a grenade and threw themselves out the second story windows of the school room. Glass, blood and moaning bodies littered the lawn. No one was dead.

Mrs. Nguyen ran from child to child, interpreting for the medics and police, reassuring the wounded and gathering those able to walk. She assembled them under a cypress tree, where they could be together, away from the white people they knew were trying to kill them again.

Emily and the Cubans showed up, driving our agency cars, still gray and still without windshields. She had called and picked up a dozen or so parents she knew had children in the school. The Cubans didn't have licenses, but Miss Emmy needed drivers and threw them the keys. They loved Miss Emmy.

The refugee parents took over from Mrs. Nguyen. She walked stiffly to the police who were interrogating the kid who threw the cherry bomb. His father was there. He had a pocket protector and a ponytail. She asked the child why he did it. He said it wasn't his fault, it was just a joke, they were just a bunch of gooks and they weren't even real Americans.

Mrs Nguyen turned and stared at the father.

"You are an animal," she said, and spat in his face. She attacked like a feral cat, all nails and teeth. The policemen pulled her off. The father did not press charges. Neither did we.

Later, Mrs. Nguyen went to the father of the young terrorist and apologized for her behavior. Then she offered me her resignation.

Emily did not like having to report to Mrs. Nguyen, the new director. Her promotion to Refugee Resettlement Coordinator with a nice raise helped ease things. They gave a nice going away party for me. Miss Emmy somehow found conga drums, guitars, and even a beat up violin. The woman is a wonder. One of the Vietnamese guys brought a yard sale mirrored disco ball and a slick Karaoke setup. The Cubans started to jam and the young Asian kids were on the dance floor doing some kind of Saigon Salsa before the mirror ball could cast its tattered beams across the parking lot. Later, the Vietnamese tore into the Karaoke like drunks on a cruise ship, doing Elvis and Sinatra with a gusto I haven't felt since my first French kiss. Mrs. Nguyen appeared in a white silk Ao Dai, the long, body hugging gown that makes Vietnamese women appear so slender and ethereal. She bowed to the audience, grabbed the mike and ripped into "I Fall to Pieces." Juan danced snaky slow in a dark corner with Miss Emmy. I slipped out around midnight. Nobody noticed. They, at least, were home.

ACE IN THE HOLE

Col. Wallace couldn't get the keys to work. War with Cuba was coming in a day or two, and his missiles wouldn't fly unless he got it right. Two men at separate consoles needed to turn the keys at the same time after a complex sequence of button pushing; even a one second difference could scotch the launch. Col. Wallace tried several of his subordinates as his partner for the firing simulations, and Lt. Johnson seemed to be his best partner. They were within three seconds of getting it right on a good trial, much worse on a bad one. If the call to pull the trigger came today, these birds were staying in the nest. This was not acceptable.

Part of the problem was construction delays. The summer had been brutal, with temperatures just under 110 degrees, and the work crews had been limited to three hour shifts. The missile silos were spread out over hundreds of square miles of barren land, fit only for a few scraggly cows and the isolated ranches of their equally scraggly owners. Spring had lasted two, maybe three days, and then winter set in. Winter comes early to the high plains of eastern Montana, and the first snow had blown in from Alberta in early October. The primary launch control center was mostly done, but a second command post was necessary to comply with activation protocols, and it would be weeks before that facility was ready. The equipment for both had been moved to the completed site, in total disregard of implementation regulations; separation of launch crews was required to avoid accidental ignition by a rogue individual.

For Col. Wallace this wasn't a big issue; he knew his men. The real problem was the key design. The female slot was located deep within a crevice on the consoles, and it was difficult to get the keys mated and turned in unison. Some genius civilian had screwed up and made the things six inches too short. Lab rats with weeks to practice could get the dance right, he guessed, but his airmen had just gotten the equipment two days before U-2 flyovers had discovered that Castro was putting up missile installations with the help of his Soviet bosses. The other Squadron Commanders hadn't come within four seconds of a successful launch simulation. Gen. Powers, their boss at Strategic Air Command, was spitting blood over the failure.

The Base Commander, Col. Spencer, called a staff meeting. New orders from Gen. Powers this morning. The President had declared DEFCON 2 for the first time in recent history. DEFCON 1 was war. The construction and training delays had stalled certification of the new solid fuel Minuteman rockets as mission ready, but most of the equipment was in place now. Gen. Powers had ordered the first flight of ten missiles armed with nukes, aimed at the Soviets and ready to fire as of yesterday. What was the god damned problem?

Col. Wallace figured the base commander was the issue. He was the second son of some tycoon in New England, raised in boarding schools and shuffled off to West Point to pursue an honorable and trust fund subsidized career, thereby avoiding inheritance conflicts with his older brother. After a World War II assignment as a public relations flack for the Army Air Corps, he transitioned into the new Air Force. Most of his service had been spent at the Pentagon briefing Generals and throwing cocktail parties. He carried a silver capped swagger stick and spoke like a Harvard Don. He had never been to war or even served in a line position. He wanted to make General; it would make Daddy proud. Wallace hated him.

When Col. Wallace suggested altering the keys, Spencer went ballistic. They were Government Issue, they were lab tested and proven reliable, this was a human failure, and Wallace better get it right before the sun set or his command was over. He would end his Air Force career at some radar station in Newfoundland.

Col. Wallace was a man who followed orders. No one made colonel without respect for the chain of command. No one with his background. Academy grads could make it on charm and connections; poor boys that got in during World War II because they took flying lessons on part time bus driver's pay while failing out of junior college had to do things well and do them by the book. There was always a book. The book was often wrong.

During the war, the young Lt. Wallace received a medal for distinguished gallantry based on an act of insubordination. While his B-17 was returning from a bombing mission over New Guinea, he spotted a pair of Japanese tankers and a destroyer anchored in a small bay. He tried to radio headquarters but couldn't get signal. Standing orders were to report such sightings and fly home, but Wallace couldn't resist the target, dropped to 50 feet and strafed the enemy ships with his 30 caliber nose turret machine gun. When he got back to his base at Port Moresby, he was relieved of duty for flagrant disregard of orders. Two days later, reconnaissance showed major fire damage to the destroyer and one of the tankers sunk. Within a week, he was back in the cockpit with a recommendation for the Silver Star, America's third highest combat honor. Things had been going badly for US forces in the Pacific so far, and the story of a young lieutenant single handedly taking on the Japanese Empire made fabulous fodder for the papers back home. You don't court martial a hero.

Wallace knew it could have gone the other way and was grateful for the second chance. He played by the book for the next twenty years, fought in Korea, moved up the ranks, and got his promotion to Colonel when he was chosen as Commander of America's first Minuteman missile squadron. They were due to go live in January, but the problem with Cuba put the pressure on to lock and load right now.

When the meeting ended, Col. Wallace sent Lt. Johnson to the launch control center and told him to prepare for more activation trials. His acid reflux had kicked in, and he swallowed a handful of calcium carbonate tablets. He always kept a few dozen in his pocket. It only took a few minutes to drive to the maintenance hangar.

Wallace had learned many useful skills as a depression farm boy. He could bail hay and butcher deer and make his dad's Model A Ford run no matter what damage it endured. Meant to be a road vehicle, his dad used it as a tractor or truck or guest room. It was the last remnant of his father's middle class aspirations before the depression killed his career and dreams. Young Wallace also learned to weld.

It took less than an hour to fuse steel extensions on the keys. Col. Wallace gunned his car as he left the base for launch control. He figured this was his career, up or down. If the keys worked, he had a chance. If not, he'd be lucky to get his pension. Altering the nuclear key would not be taken lightly.

Col. Spencer and Lt. Johnson were there when he arrived. Col. Wallace told Spencer what he had done. The vein on Spencer's forehead started to pulse, but all he said was "noted." He stood in the corner silently as the two men ran through the launch procedure. Johnson couldn't get the newly configured key into the slot in time.

They ran the procedure again. When it came time for final ignition, Col. Wallace took the key from Lt. Johnson and stood between the consoles. He glanced at Spencer standing silently with his arms crossed. He spread his arms and inserted both keys into their slots and turned them. The display said it was a go.

Col. Spencer picked up the phone.

"General Powers, this is Burt Spencer. You can tell President Kennedy his missiles are a go. Thank you,

Sir."

He turned to Col. Wallace as he exited the bunker. "Don't leave until it takes two people to make this bastard fly."

President Kennedy told Khrushchev his ace in the hole was armed and ready to go. The Soviets backed down. Three days later America was back to DEFCON 3; the bombers were called back, the missiles stood down, the nukes deinstalled, and the post action review teams were out at every operational base. The results were embarrassing. At one point in time, one man without orders could have set off World War III. Col. Spencer was sent to Hungary as Air Attaché to the American Embassy. His father would not be proud.

What to do with Col. Wallace was a problem. Gen. Powers wanted to promote him for his ingenuity, but knew that if word got out about the incident it would be a political nightmare. The man had to be buried far away from any media snoops. There was a new and nasty little war starting up in Vietnam. Wallace was quietly transferred to a bomber unit running secret missions over Cambodia. Very hush hush.

THE ROAD TO OLD FORGE

The roof had been falling in for a week. I propped it up with a two by four, but the rain found a way through and dripped on a corner of the mattress. Luckily, it wasn't a real bed, just a crappy thrift store hand-me-down futon of lumpy, mildewed cotton on top of squeaky rusted box springs lying on the floor. I pushed it across the room, away from the torrent, and called the landlord again. Again, the landlord said he'd fix it tomorrow.

The landlord has hated us since Ronnie brought the goat home. She figured she could feed it on leaves and such from the yard. It jumped the fence the first night and ate the neighbor's newly planted garden. The neighbor was the landlord's niece. Ronnie argued with him for a week or so, even offered him some homemade cheese as a bribe, but the landlord was adamant that the goat must go. Ronnie sold the animal to a nearby commune at a loss, and brought home a barking dog. So much for maintenance.

I was late for work, but had to do something about the water. I called Jim down at dispatch. Things were slow, but I needed to be in my cab by nine, when the bar hopper trade started to heat up. I went to the shed looking for some container to catch the water. I could hear Ronnie in the house, cranking up an old Stones album. "Bitch" came on at volume nine. She was in the bedroom sopping up the water with a towel and singing along when I came back with a bucket. I put it under the leak and left for work. Ronnie smiled and said goodbye.

Tonight, while I was hauling drunks from bar to bar, she would be fucking my best friend Freddy. She told me this at dinner. She had married too young. She had never been with another man. She needed to find her sexual self, and good as I was, I was not enough. I shouldn't worry because because because. She'd be there when I got home. She cleared the table and lit a joint and then the rain began again, a real Adirondack thunder buster. It would be a perfect night for the taxi trade.

I picked up my cab from the company garage and headed for the liquor store, always the first stop at the beginning of my shift. It was the only place you could get hard stuff, and it closed at ten. I got a case of vodka and another of cheap whiskey and stowed them in the trunk. Most of the bars closed at one in the morning and the late bars closed at two. After that, I was the bartender. Alcoholics are cheap bastards, but they always have enough for one more bottle after the watering holes have shut down. I charged at least double my cost, sometimes more. Cabbies can't make it on tips alone.

There wouldn't be much action until midnight, so I parked in front of the bus station and pulled out the new *Playboy*. I was too upset by the Ronnie thing and couldn't get into it. I'm all for free love and love the one you're with and share the love and such, but I wanted a goddamned wife, not an earth mother, and I was pissed. At least she was open about it, but I didn't feel like much of a man. As for Freddy, he could kiss my ass.

A bus came in from Albany, but only one guy got off. He looked old and worthless, with baggy eyes and a saggy mackinaw and a small duffle bag that looked half empty. He walked right up and asked me to take him to the nearest bar. I asked to see his money. He pulled a wad of crumpled bills out of his coat pocket and threw them on the front seat and asked if that would cover me. There was at least a hundred, maybe two. Four nights pay in this cheap shit upstate town. He pulled a pint of scotch out of the other pocket, polished it off, and asked if I would stick with him for a few hours. He intended to get smashed, and didn't want to fool around with a bunch of strangers. He threw another twenty on the seat. I called dispatch and told Jim I had a hot one; take me off the call list. I told the old guy I was his boy.

His name was Harry and he was a fishing boat captain in Maine; had been, at least. He'd sold his boat to a man in Bar Harbor, cashed the check, stuffed a hundred thousand in his duffle, and caught a bus for the Adirondacks. I suggested we stow the money bag in the trunk; he agreed. I brought my new best friend a fresh bottle of whiskey.

Harry wanted to go to a working man's bar, a place where he could raise some hell and not get thrown out. I took him to Millie's down in south Plattsburgh. That's where the loggers and construction guys went to shoot pool and get in fights. Millie had a bat under the cash register for real assholes, but generally let altercations play themselves out. The regular clientele knew the rules, and the cops were afraid to mess with Millie and what she called her boys.

I parked the cab and took Harry directly to Millie. She liked him right off. Millie was in her sixties, weighed around 300 pounds, and had a mouth like an outhouse. Harry was skinny as a shit stick and spoke the same language. If either one was still capable of sex, they'd have done it right there on the bar. As it was, Harry ordered Canadian Club, double shot, and watched the boys play pool. I told him I had some business to take care of, and wondered if I could leave for a half hour or so. Harry said fine and went over to shoot some eight ball.

I drove home and parked in the alley. Freddy's car was out front. I could see candle light dancing against the curtains; the Doors were on the stereo. I went to the shed and fetched my deer rifle; Ronnie wouldn't let me keep it in the house. Good thing. I kicked in the bedroom door as "This is the End" came on and fired off two quick rounds.

The record player exploded. The other bullet missed Ronnie by three inches and tore up the down pillow propped under her butt. Feathers filled the air like snow. Missed is the wrong word; I never miss. It went where I put it. Freddy jumped up all shivery and freaked out and backed his skinny ass into the closet. His dick had shriveled to the size of a jelly bean. I motioned him out the door with the tip of the gun. He didn't try to grab his clothes, just ran buck naked into the night. Ronnie curled up in a fetal position and hyper-ventilated. I put the gun away in the shed and drove back to Millie's.

Harry was having a fine time. He'd won a couple hundred from some of the young loggers and spent it all buying the house drinks. Everybody was calling him Gramps and slapping his back. I figured he'd found his home for the night and would stay until they closed, but he waved me over and told me it was time to leave.

He wanted to go to Old Forge, more than a few hours away on the other side of the Park. I asked him what was there. He said he saw it on a map before he left Maine, and it sounded like a good place to die. Nobody would know him or care, and he was ready. I gassed up the cab, called dispatch to let Jim know where I was going, and headed down Highway 3. Harry curled up in the back seat and sucked on his bottle. Every fifteen or so minutes he'd belch and babble and throw another handful of money into the front seat.

I contemplated dumping his body in the woods somewhere north of Blue Mountain Lake. The hundred grand in the trunk could take this cabbie a long way, and after all, Harry wanted to die someplace where no one knew him. I was pretty depressed by the home scene, and this could be my magical free pass out of Ronnie land. I was looking for a turnoff down some dirt log road, but we came up on Saranac Lake and passed a tavern that was still open. Harry asked me to pull over.

The bar was dead. Harry got a six pack of beer to go and we headed out to the cab. He asked me to fetch the money bag from the trunk. When we got back on the road, he tossed three bundles of twenties on to the front seat and thanked me for sticking with him. How can you kill a guy like that?

We got to Old Forge at five in the morning. Harry was passed out in the back seat. The only place open was Walt's Diner, so I hauled Harry in and dumped him in a booth. I asked the waitress if they had a cab in this dinkum town and she called a guy. When he arrived, I gave him a hundred and told him to take good care of my boy. Call me a god-damned fool, but I left the duffle with Harry.

I got home around nine in the morning. Ronnie was frying up some bacon and eggs. She had cleaned herself and the house up, and was as bright and smiley as a fucking TV weather lady. She asked me how the rest of the night went. Average, I said, and dug into breakfast.

EPILOGUE:

THE ACCIDENTAL TOURON

In Arizona, they have a derogatory name for people who come and stay just for the winter months: Snowbird. If you can hang on for a full year, sweat like the locals through a summer of dust storms and a hundred plus days of 100^0 plus temperatures, most folks consider you a native. Most folks, however, came from somewhere else, and it is relatively easy to be accepted. After two decades in the Southwest sun, I had become a proud desert rat. If some rookie asked me how I took the brutal summers, I would smile enigmatically and say that it was the best time of year. All the Snowbirds were gone.

Then, in 2004, my wife Leslie and I inherited a house in Lake Placid. She had been coming to the Adirondacks since she was five and had numerous friends in town, but I knew no one. We were at the point in our lives where we were thinking about a summer place in the mountains. The High Peaks were a long way from Arizona, but fate had placed them before us, and we decided to spend three months in the North Country during the summer of 2005.

It was my first week in town. I was trying to drive through the crowded tourist district to pick up some bagels, but traffic was blocked in both directions. Lake Placid was full of people who had come for the 4th of July holiday, and all the vehicles I could see had license plates from Massachusetts, Connecticut, New

Jersey, Vermont, Quebec. Some of the motorists had double parked, some were reading maps with their doors half open into traffic, some were screaming out of their car windows at the worst of the drivers. Three cars ahead of me, a truck towing a trailer tried to pull into a municipal parking lot, but got stuck in mid turn when another car backed into the street and blocked his way. I had had enough. There was a brief opening in oncoming traffic because of the jam up, and I made a quick and screeching U-turn and headed out of town. As I pulled away, I heard a pedestrian scream at me.... "Touron!!!"

That night we had dinner with Kay and Ed, born and bred in the Tri-Lakes, true locals of the highest water. I told them my experience downtown and asked what a Touron was. After laughing up great chunks of half swallowed chili, they told me it meant "tourist moron." I asked what other names there were for people like me: shoobie, leaf peeper, masshole, joey, tourorist. Apparently, the best you could be was a "seasonal," someone who came back every year for the summer and left when the air got chill.

I have traveled the world and been insulted in at least a dozen languages, but this one hurt the most. In my few short days here, the magic of the Adirondacks had already begun to invade my spirit. It wasn't just the beauty. As a young man, I had written a play, had it produced, got an agent, and started a career as a TV writer. Life (and two children) interfered with my creative instincts, and I spent the next few decades securing a more stable life for my family. I had taught college in the US and Iran, worked in refugee camps in Southeast Asia and Central America, been a manager in the computer industry, and, with my wife, started a tour company in Arizona that took people all over the world. Now, as I settled into the North Country, I could sense my artistic juices beginning to flow again. I loved the feeling and wanted acceptance in my new part time home, not the label of an outsider who was "from away," "not from here." I wanted to fit in and stretch my wings.

Unfortunately, I have always been a man who isolates. If you saw me at a party, I'd be the one back in the shadows in the farthest corner of the room, watching the action and taking mental notes. Approach me and I would be polite but say little of interest or nothing at all. You would find me to be boring. At home, I spent most of my time in front of my computer surfing the net and listening to the radio, or writing poems I never shared with anyone and living entirely in my head. It took an act of Congress to get me off my duff and out the door.

Or so it was until that horrid day in Lake Placid, when I made a decision that has changed my life, a decision to seek out a new kind of relationship with the world. I went to the local tourist office and got a copy of The Weekender, a listing of all the cultural activities going on in the High Peaks. I marked every concert and art opening and theater performance and went to every event I could. Because this is a small community, I started to see the same people over and over. Because I wanted to change, I sucked it up and stuck out my hand and introduced myself. Because I appeared far more confident than I felt, I was somehow invited to hike or dine with the people I met. We left for Arizona in early fall.

Each year we came back a bit earlier and stayed a bit longer. We bought kayaks and learned to paddle. The grandkids came to visit and became friends with the neighbor's kids. People recognized us at social events and welcomed us back. By 2010, we were spending six months here and six months in Arizona. We had become accepted "seasonals."

New friends gave me occasional grief about being a wimp regarding winter. I hadn't spent a season in the snow since High School in Great Falls, Montana. I knew what 40^0 below felt like, and didn't feel up to abandoning the Arizona sunshine for blizzards and black ice. Still, the mountains were feeling more and more like home and the desert southwest more like a place to escape rather than a place to enjoy. I decided to get more involved, and took a part time job teaching online courses for North Country Community College in Saranac Lake. That allowed me to keep in contact with my new favorite place while I was away. I boldly told my Tri-Lakes buddies that, given a proper excuse, I might just spend a winter here, just to prove I could do it.

In August of 2010, the "proper excuse" came along. A week before the fall semester began at NCCC, an English Professor quit. I was asked if I could stay and fill in. I took a deep breath, abandoned my sanity, and said yes. I asked my neighbor how she had survived up here for so many years. She said you had to embrace the winter, seek it out, actively engage with it. Otherwise, you would become cabin bound and spend all your time cranky and alone. I stocked up on winter clothes, borrowed skis and snowshoes, and dug my daddy's ancient arctic parka out of storage. I opened the door and walked out face first into the snowiest and coldest Adirondack winter in twenty years. The Weekender was my guide to cold weather activities, as it had been to summer fun.

In the last six months I have seen seven plays, attended fifteen art openings, participated in thirteen literary readings, and squatted with my brethren at eleven meditation group sessions. I have heard music in half a dozen venues, met with actors and directors at a film forum, and been lectured by master gardeners, who taught me how to create a grow room in my basement and came by to make sure I actually did it. I have learned to snow shoe and ski and answer the phone without checking to see who or what is calling. I have hiked and kayaked with people who think of me as a friend. When I go to the grocery store, folks say hello and know my name. I acquired a New York driver's license and changed my legal residency to Lake Placid.

Last week I went to visit the historical society housed in the Lake Placid train station. In one corner was a display about the old Lake Placid Club, originally founded in 1895 to provide a summer playground for the rich and famous from the great cities of the east coast. One plaque said that, in 1920, six members of the club decided to promote the area as a destination for winter sports. On the adjacent wall was a large blue flag with a white bird in the center. It was the original Sno Bird, seeking rather than fleeing winter. I had come full circle. No longer a "seasonal," I am home.

About the author

Early in his career, Charles Watts had an underground play ("Visigoths") produced in Los Angeles, which led to script writing contracts for several TV series. He fled Hollywood, got an MFA in poetry, and went to Iran to teach literature. For five years, he edited Seizure, a magazine of poetry and fiction. He has been a cab driver, worked in refugee camps in Southeast Asia and Central America, and owned a tour company. He has published stories and poems in a broad range of literary journals. "Karma in the High Peaks," an anthology from Ra Press that included ten of his poems, won the "People's Choice Award" for best book of 2010 from the Adirondack Center for Writing.

www.ingramcontent.com/pod-product-compliance
Lightning Source LLC
Chambersburg PA
CBHW031844170626
46807CB00004B/1619